FLOWER

Ed Atkins is a British artist based in Copenhagen. He is best known for realistic computer-generated videos that expose and scrutinize otherwise unavailable feelings by the profanity of their artifice. In recent years he has presented solo shows at Kunsthaus Bregenz, Martin-Gropius-Bau in Berlin, Castello di Rivoli in Turin, the Stedelijk Museum in Amsterdam and Serpentine Gallery in London, among others, with a survey show at Tate Britain opening in spring 2025. *Flower* is his first work of non-fiction and his third book with Fitzcarraldo Editions after *A Primer for Cadavers* (2016) and *Old Food* (2019).

'I feel like a permanent conduit has been built between my brain and this book. Atkins is relentless, beautiful, hideously and angelically honest. Sometimes it brought me to tears and I'm not even sure why. It's the stuff most of us leave out, or wouldn't even know how to articulate. By which I mean this book has made so much other writing feel like propaganda. It's heroic. I'm not sure I'll ever recover from it.'
— Luke Kennard, author of *Notes on the Sonnets*

'Every sentence in this delightfully bizarre techno-memoir could stand alone on a page and command allure. Like splicing the miniature divulgences of Édouard Levé with the ominous bombast of Jenny Holzer, *Flower* makes automatic non-fiction feel like sci-fi, and it's instantly unforgettable.'
— Blake Butler, author of *Molly*

'*Flower* is propulsive and it doesn't let up. It's about vulnerability, sort of, and invincibility: it swings between these poles. It's about mortality, too, and in that sense humanity. To speak the book back at itself, I confess it did get to me.'
— Isabel Waidner, author of *Corey Fah Does Social Mobility*

'You might say Ed Atkins is an old-school modernist. Like Joyce or Woolf, his writing tracks the human mind grappling with consciousness, moment-to-moment. But they never watched it grappling with clammy wraps and smartphones. *Flower* is funny, confessional, futuristic, hypnotic, suffused with love and loss and drizzled in fizzy cola. I read Atkins to learn how writing can be made new all over again.'
— Dan Fox, author of *Pretentiousness: Why it Matters*

'In its hysterical representation of Ed's demonic internalities, *Flower* surfs waves of experiencing typically suppressed, bypassed, ignored. What seems at first blush exemplary of contemporary literary modes of postmodern confession quickly cumulates into a free mobility of avid, jagged distraction at a comic-book clip as his exaggeratedly magnified self-awareness refracts and distends. A rhythmically unique flow and a robust "minor work" in the best possible sense: file *Flower*'s barrage of Ed's "sexless kinks" under New Forms Of Poetry.'
— Zach Phillips, Fievel is Glauque

'Suppurations of the skin, disturbances of the gut, tender feelings, weird appetites, love, disgust, prayer: the unbroken paragraph of *Flower* is a delirious, frenetic, exhilarating voyage through the crevices and byways of a mind and a body, redolent by turns of Woolf, Beckett, Bernhard and yet like nothing I've ever read.'
— Josh Cohen, author of *All the Rage*

'Bubbling over with sensation, *Flower* revels in the pleasures of incoherence and the wondrous terror of being alive. Atkins uses relentless self-exposure to turn his flesh inside out, revealing its viscera, gunk and goop. A striking and moving exploration of direct experience, Atkins renders the body as a biological machine and site of existential struggle.'
— Martine Syms

'Finally someone is writing about all the food in drugstores. A paean of appreciation to these freakish purveyors of junk is how Atkins launches his amorous, granular unspooling of outrageous drives and appetites. *Flower* is the kind of book many people dream of writing: kudos to Atkins for getting it on the page.'
— Moyra Davey, author of *Index Cards*

'Ed Atkins is a radical humanist who rediscovers the human in the most inhuman of states, when the usual supports – ego, language, people, technology, media, food – all fail. In *Flower* Atkins turns that abjection towards us, in a spleeny anti-autofiction that is his own version of *Les Fleurs du Mal*.'
—— Hal Foster, author of *What Comes After Farce?*

Praise for *Old Food*

'Violent, emetic, immoderate, improper, impure – that's to say it's the real thing. Atkins' prose, which may not be prose, adheres to Aragon's maxim "Don't think – write."'
—— Jonathan Meades

'Ed Atkins is the artist of ugly feelings – gruesome and smeared and depleted. But everything he does in his videos or paintings, I've always thought, he really does as a writer. He uses language as a system where everything gets reprocessed and misshapen – a unique and constant mislaying of tone that's as dizzying as it's exhilarating.'
—— Adam Thirlwell, author of *The Future Future*

'Reading like the accelerated brain patterns of a ravenous soothsayer-cum-scavenger-cum-time-travellingsalesperson, auto-translated into an almost recognizable diction, *Old Food* tastes of sick period drama, nostalgic for a time just around the corner. As singular as electrocution, it emits from the demented ditches, the euphoric crusts, disappointed hearts and bad gut-feelings as much as the patterned constellations, throbbing with multidimensional love-songs. From inside these erotic and squalid operatics, Ed Atkins revamps the scene of our selves. His writing advances like a daredevil knife-thrower, nervy and elastic, spinning words at the reader's throat.'
—— Heather Phillipson, author of *Whip-hot & Grippy*

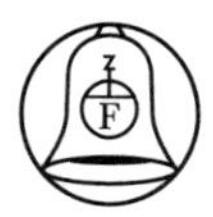

Fitzcarraldo Editions

FLOWER

ED ATKINS

For Sally-Ginger

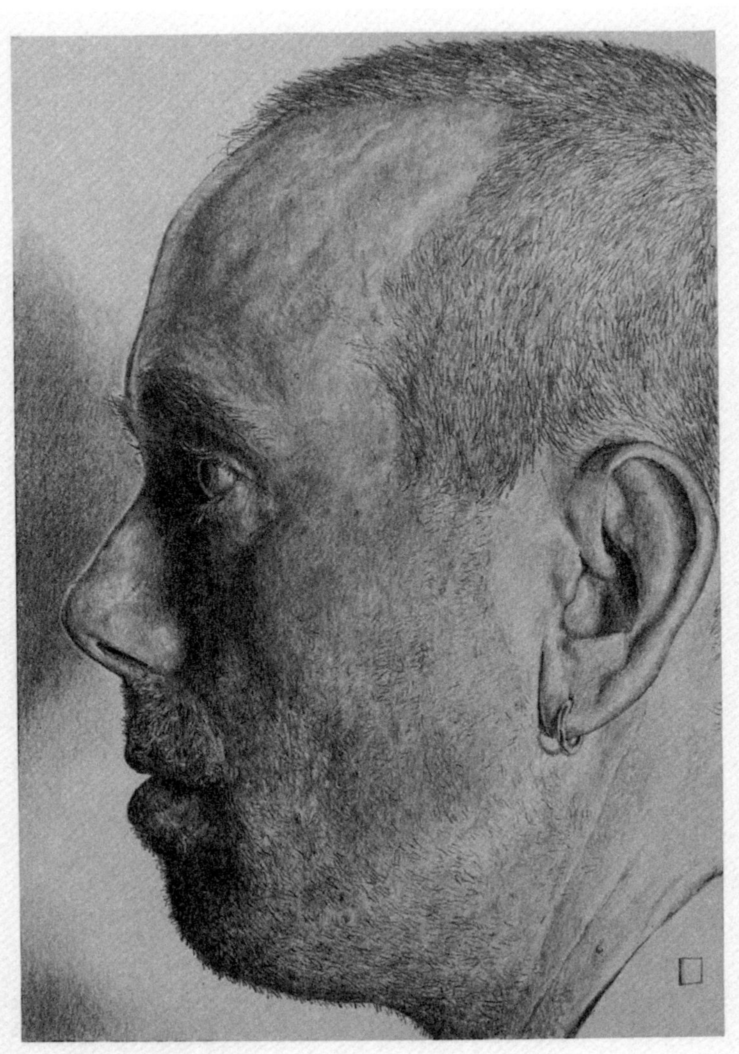

'Soft drinks can be classified into three categories:
Cola flavored, fruit flavored, or citrus flavored. The
colas, like Coke or Pepsi, are the favorite among real
connoisseurs. Ther is nothing like a cola to pick one
up or refresh one on a hot day.'
— Simon Thompson, *Bluestone*

I like eating cold, clammy wraps from big pharmacies that are open late and sell just a few foods like protein bars and powders. I like wraps near the skin creams, neoprenes and scrunchies. I also like the wraps they sell in cheap supermarkets and franchise corner shops and mid-tier garages. The cheap supermarket near me sells just a few lunch things they don't have an obvious lunch bit. The few wraps they do sell are really close to the tills, seemingly on the wrong side of the tills you have to know they're there otherwise when you do see them it's probably on the way out, too late to think to buy one. I like wraps fabricated on industrial estates a long way from here that come in nondescript cardboard and plastic sleeves. I won't register what's inside the wraps I like it doesn't matter at all. The best wraps all taste the same: sweet creamed hospice. The wraps I like are best and look like these spent prophylactic alien larvae props. I push them through my mouth. The best wraps are always presented in half with the two halves side-by-side in the sleeve. The cut ends of it are cut on the bias and are on prominent display behind the plastic window at the top of the package. The visible cross-section is not at all instructive. The damp folded ends are hidden in the cardboard bottom like its genitals. This differs from the wraps I tend not to like which are detailed. They have purples and dark greens in. They are performatively healthy and aspirational. These wraps tend to be presented halved with the halves end-to-end rather than side-by-side in the packaging and their ingredients are conspicuously discrete. The cut ends of the wrap are straight and are hidden behind a cardboard centre bit where the label is. Instead, I like the pharmacy ones where it's satisfying and you can see the striation. There's usually a bit of wet stuff on the inside of the see-through plastic where the wrap's touched the plastic in transit. I think buying a wrap in a pharmacy is incredible. I once bought a huge wrap in a Walgreens in Manhattan. It came with a sachet of extra mayonnaise tucked into the packaging even though it was already heavy with mayonnaise. I bought it and a thin can of Coke Zero and ate and drank while walking, like an actor. It's usually a kind of chicken prep inside the wraps I like but it's so unrecognizable to the mouth and the eye as to be moot, the name, the food question, and likewise the preparation who knows. A wrap is chopped foods folded up in a bib of par-cooked very flatbread. Once folded up it looks like a handmade food tube with hospital corners at the ends to stop the food tumbling out when it's lifted vertical to eat. I eat it, or someone else eats it, and thinks of drastic things coolly. The best wraps are cavefish and peter forever outside time. That goes for a lot of what's happening when I'm inside of a big pharmacy. I feel out-side of time and outside of my life. I go in to a big pharmacy when it's dark outside. I buy a wrap and a fizzy drink with my earbuds in listening to my music. My music lends the whole thing a cinematic thing. I'm the crushed protagonist buying a corpse-like wrap and a thin can of Coke Zero on another planet the same as this one. I'll take my earbuds out to pay unless there's a self-checkout. A self-checkout's good for buying food at the pharmacy. The fantasy ennobles whatever and lifts what from the outside looks miserable but is not. When I have food in that's bad for me I'll bolt some of it then bin the rest and pour bleach over it in the bin so I can't fish it out later and eat it, then. I'll smoke the first cigarette from a new pack then go to the sink and hold the rest of the pack under the cold tap on full or I'll have a first few pulls on a cigarette and pluck it from my mouth and flick it some irretrievable place. The expression on my face won't change; when there's no one around I needn't be convincing. This is very realistic; my feelings happen internally. I'll have half a glass from a bottle of wine then upend the rest of the bottle into the sink. I like making whatever bad thing irredeemable because I don't trust future me to be consistent with current me. I know I'm inconsistent and this can be frightening. Self-love is an unobservable phenomenon that cavils forever. I should be punished but not killed outright. I bought a big bag of Doritos in Blackheath in the morning and started eating them in rough stacks outside the shop. I then sharpish turned and emptied the rest into a bin there and used the empty Dorito bag as a shiny mitt to force the Doritos deep into the bin, then. Everything else in the bin groaned and shifted downward. When I'm alone I'll buy processed foods and unrefrigerated pre-mixed alcoholic drinks. Once, my mouth was full of Dorito pulp and room-temperature vodka maracujá drink outside a späti in Berlin in the summer, great. Cool Original Doritos have a remarkable savoury flavour I can't place. The bag has a lot of blue and black on it, as well as dramatic photos of the Doritos. Blue and black are inedible executive colours. They mark the contents as exclusive and ambitious. I think it's Cool Ranch flavour in the US, a thick dressing. I like processing Doritos with my mouth. Saliva piddles moisten while molars pound to a paste. I compress the paste between my tongue and the roof of my mouth to make now Dorito-flavoured and coloured spit leach from it and get into me via ducts. The paste remainder forms a curved cast and this is a remarkable temporary food object. I cut the soft cast object into neat nothings with my teeth then and swallow it easily. I'm just getting rid of shapes down a chute. The thing we all go to Doritos for is the intense flavour and astonishing colour. Dorito flavour is staggering.

It can be easily decoupled from the corn medium inside my mouth. The flavour and the colour of Doritos cheers me up no end and the lurid smut on my fingers. I like eating all kinds of cheese puffs. They don't pique my loathsomeness much as they're just aerated packing material, a deniable foodstuff at the far end of edible. I eat cheese puffs with an urgency that from the outside looks like mechanical efficiency but isn't it's just noise in me, it's squirming almost nothing perhaps pleasure's dust there's nothing to it. The cheese flavour of cheese puffs varies within a small window only, whereas actual real cheeses have many different ones. When an ideal of course ghosts I toss the future after it. Silk Cuts are okay when they're customized: cover over the perforations with a torn-off glue strip from a cigarette paper or you can clamp two fingers over the perforations while you smoke to make it proper strength. I do something similar with my vape nowadays. I part-block a valve near the mouthpiece of the vape with my fingertip and in this way I can throttle the vapour. The vape mouthpiece is musical-feeling, like a child's first wind instrument. Stuff from my mouth and lips comes off on the mouthpiece and can gather in the breathing hole but I can always get a pin or a sharp pencil and gouge the stuff out and wipe it on a trouser leg. I keep the vape in one of my two trouser pockets. Sharp lint from my pocket can get in the breathing hole and shoot into my unsuspecting throat when I vape it. I like vaping all of the time. My vape provides me with my home planet's gas mix without which otherwise I'd suffocate on Earth's mix. As with my voice my exhalation made visible by vape in it is an aspect of me that flees me to be with the world and never to return. I like that there's formaldehyde in vapes but I don't like popcorn lung. When the juice runs out I taste burning metal. When the juice leaks

18

into your mouth sometimes oh, it's very obviously poison I'm pulling in. I know about formaldehyde from alien foetuses and big decapitated heads in jars of it but I don't know about popcorn lung. It's a very evocative name and an ominously fun euphemism I won't look up the reality of. I secretly vape on planes, in cinemas, in concert halls; everywhere you can't vape you can actually very easily vape without discovery. I palm the vape like an inmate. I ensure the little glowing display's hidden. I look straight at anyone nearby so if they try looking at me they'll be met by my gaze before they see that I'm vaping so that they'll immediately look away. This sort of pre-emptive gaze is weird, it repulses others' sight; it relies on being there first, looking first, and on protocol. I pull on the vape and hold it in for as long as possible so that the vapour dissipates in me. By the time I breathe out there's no giveaway vape opaquing my breath. In circumstances where vaping's not really okay to do I take care to pull on it when I'm quite sure it won't be my turn to talk or laugh for about twenty seconds, which is about how long the vape takes to entirely dissipate in me. During this time I smile and nod while I hold it in. I can do it. I presume it's fine to vape everywhere or I don't care if it is or it isn't. I have the gall to do it in someone else's house just in front of everyone mid-conversation without asking. If someone says something I feel terribly guilty. I feel for myself via remembered stilled machines still warm to the touch. I'm shadowing myself through a history of my own impersonal sentimentality the pining for which electroplates the meaningless with a rose zirconium-like. I sat alone on a low stool at a low table in a pub lounge and customized a Silk Cut. The table and the stool were genuinely small. There was an empty blue glass ashtray and a drained pint glass marbled with beer foam scum on the

small table which was round and of a brown metal spack-
led with little hammered divots. My hands are seen from
an instructional isometric perspective and my concen-
trating face is in close-up which in this sequence bravely
allows it the ugly repose of the unobserved. I gave an
unaffected performance with my jaw slackened. I bulged
some. No visible musculature and no visible veining on
my arms. What was I? I'd a pad of green Rizla, a purple
and white Silk Cut ten-pack and a black plastic lighter
with a silver cuff. I got a cigarette paper and tore the glue
strip off it. I licked the glue strip and wrapped it around
one Silk Cut's midriff to dress the perforations that make
it healthy, closed. Then I took up the lighter and ground
the striking wheel slowly with my thumb, moving the
lighter up and down just above the Silk Cut, milling
invisible flint bits over it. Then I smoked the Silk Cut and
the flint bits once caught spat glum sparks when the lit tip
was on them. The sparkles and the blued smoke dawdling
around my head made my head look like a monument to
something on the night of its national holiday. This was
when you could smoke inside pubs in the UK which is
when this part is set. When I run out of cigarettes I collect
the squashed butts from the ashtray, split them open
along the middle with my thumbnail like minnows, and
empty the stinky spent tobacco into a new cigarette paper
to smoke. The catch when smoke goes haltingly past my
epiglottis is abject but I could be wrong to use those words
– abject, epiglottis. The catch resumes disbelief and with
it my body happens in my embrace by myself of it. I know
it's a turnstile, I know it admits smoke or not, I know it's
not the pink teardrop. People start smoking for different
reasons. I started smoking when I was twelve I rolled
Tony and his flunkies cigarettes at Sophie's party in a
barn in Wootton and everyone drenched in Lynx or

Impulse. I slipped away and walked home when the little brick of Golden Virginia ran out, purposeless. I often walked the many miles home through the countryside in the middle of the night as a teenager, blank I can't remember feeling anything. There was no one else anywhere. We'd two welcome paedophiles in the village. Jim had no toes but I loved acting. The image of my future radicalizes and pillories my present. I abuse myself in ways. I like eating tinned hot dog sausages drooped onto sliced white, scribbled with ketchup. I like the iron-blood taste of tinned hot dog sausages and their cold makes them seem found, eaten speculatively. I like modelling balloons pumped with blood meal, it seems. Hot dog sausages are a more appetizing prospect than recognizable meats if you're like me. I eat ultra-processed meat products as a cannibal. The main ingredient in ultra-processed meats is the ultra-processing, the ultra-processing's culture and its technologies and histories rather than the beautiful pig in the past. Cannibalism is the correct way to be. I like eating indexed human technology. The things I like eating the most are moulded from appalling civilizational expression, then, and hot dog sausages are teeming mud with robot the homogeneous. I'm a basic model cyborg out on the street with bits dangling off. Segments of my body are metal plates but meat-buffered so don't make direct contact with one another so you can't tell I'm a cyborg. When I pass you there's no screech of metal on metal. I'm mechanical but what old sound possesses my mechanism predates smelting. I like the advert for a cosmetic black gum a person smears across their nose and chin I saw on Instagram. When the black gum sets, fingers come in and peel it off and with it come plugs of off-white stuff tugged from the pores and shown to the camera. It's very convincing; get that stuff out with the black gum. Chris showed us a really great YouTube video of a dude inhaling hot dog sausages like he was a pneumatic tube system. Another advert I like has a dentist's hook chipping panes of butter-yellow plaque from the base of some front bottom teeth in close-up in CG. My teeth are not good. I haven't visited the dentist in over ten years I'm 41 right now. I have not seen a doctor in thirty years. I think it's an anniversary of neglect. I have a decade old sandwich in Tupperware on a shelf in the studio. I can't remember what was in the sandwich I have had it so long it came with me from Berlin. I had another sandwich in a sandwich bag pinned to the cork-board in my bedroom when I was a child. At the end of the day it looked like dark wet wool in a bag. Sally says she likes my teeth. 'They're colourful,' she says euphemistically. The last time I went to the dentist the hygienist cleaned my teeth angrily. My gums bled a lot and they told me to make an appointment on the way out to come back in six months to have my wisdom teeth pulled and some fillings done maybe more things done. The leading expression of good spirits is a good smile. This makes teeth burdened bones and under such duress I wonder if the misery of knackered teeth manifests its literal cringe. So lips schtummed over the evidence symptomatically gives glum, which makes a person eventually inevitably glum. I don't like being scolded for not looking after myself because of course they're right but it foils my divine aspect, which encases me in a sweet brittle sugar-work. When I finally go to the dentist they look agog, then resigned, and then grave. They sink back into their pleather dentist's chair and tug off their mask. They sigh deeply. They say, I'm afraid we're going to have to wrench them all out of it and operate on your jaw bones now. I hope there will be the option of having the new fake ones be golden ones. The last time I went to the doctor he tugged at my testicles roughly. It was actually a suspected torsion of the testicles it was okay in the end. At the hospital I was left to decide whether they should go in and take a look after a lot of healthcare professionals had fondled my testicles because the ultrasounds were inconclusive. I take ibuprofen and paracetamol at the same time. Ibuprofen shrinks swollen things and paracetamol calms angry things but neither will cure you of it. I like using a fast-acting ibuprofen drug called Nurofen Express liqui-caps the most. They're red jellied torpedoes. Branded painkillers work best on me. Placebos of brand identity and price-hike go well with who I am. The stock I place in how something looks, how effortful and costly the design and manufacture seem, is quite indicative of who I am. However cheap it might seem to use decors to bolster me it's what I do. I am cheap according to a notion of wealth as to mean richness and depth of character. It's not that I am not deep or rich in character but that apart from the allotted holes only the top layer or so of me is available to me for corroboration without incision. My being and my body are in agreement regarding my lack of depth and if the first one is metaphor and the second literal I may as well stick with the second because at night I can gently depress my thigh or I can budge my genitals and confirm that I am. I spend a hugely long time deciding how to arrange some flowers when we have them. I like to buy Nurofen Express liqui-caps when I buy painkillers in the UK. They're darling and they work, what can I say. They're scientifically engineered to kill pain faster and the red of them is for an urgency I can't muster. They absolutely torpedo pain that I couldn't have found myself in me; there's a target printed on the box in shades of heat. They lock on to pain and: zap it down.

Cars move back and forth and helicopters go up and down. Painkillers shuttle so quickly down tunnels by the efforts of my puce heart's pumps and the shape of the painkiller. It's costly to make silver and gold boxes with debossed text and powerful infographics on. I can't think of myself as a sports car but I am calmed if I can think of myself as an old robot with a combustion engine in it, puttering. I want to be fixable and my parts replaceable with whatever's to hand. I want to be precise and ad hoc to others as a thing. I work better with intervention for sure but I don't know what I am. My insides are cogs and gears and cams clicking and ticking in lovely meter and ideally there are black rubber hoses connecting it all up. It's all slick and slippy with lubricant and it all glistens seductively when my headlamp sweeps across it. I move jerkily forward in a debt shape, which defines my weak sense of achievement. I am uninterested in esoteric forms of pain-killing. I think having an interest in something is important if that thing is going to do it. I am several semantically distinct kinds of materialist. The more esoteric the therapy the more it requires belief and will. I must have health happen to me. If a therapy promises something achievable only by diligence it won't work. Any failure is more guilt and the same is true of learning. I wish I were tenderly piloted from a thousand miles away by a figure. I wish I had one of Tony Conrad's cork-board paintings with the big white incontinence pants pinned to it. A headache moves out from the culprit and mulches foxes in eddies of time-lapse. Flowers swoon and shrivel in fanning circles but it's unclear whether the headache ripples lose power the further out they get or if they go on at the same power forever. All heads will droop. Nurofen Express liqui-caps defibrillate or scream like fireworks up my hollow. They explode near the corrugated roof in sequin valentine showers of blood over nerve nubs and stadiums of faeces. Most things I like and want to be around are plasticky toy things like me. I have always liked: miniaturization like most people. I immerse chalky or oversized painkiller tablets into spoonfuls of yoghurt to get them past my gag reflex. I came up with this when I was very young. It's because my body knows you just gollop safe yoghurt and my epiglottis will open happily for it, whereas a big pill isn't right so I slip it in the yoghurt and it slips past my defences, hidden in the yoghurt and I get the effect of the painkiller and some yoghurt. The second-hand toy shop near me is a heaven. Rummaging through buckets of forsaken toy misc I can choose an inch-high perished pink rubber boot, say, or a very small harpoon or a dulled plastic goblet or a cream bonnet where the weave is clogged moulded plastic. Each from a different toy line now marooned to exquisiteness. My nominative jewels. I recently bought: a two-inch Robocop without its helmet and one leg off; a tiny black ape with its arms raised in anger and just a red mouth; a paint-chipped die-cast Matchbox car with a moustachioed head poking up through the sunroof wearing a pickelhaube; an alien purple plastic ramp with sockets along one edge to affix it to a missing stretch of purple road; and a purple plastic ghoul whose mouth ratchets open like a mantrap so if you press down on its bumpy red tongue with your finger the mouth snaps shut suddenly. The teeth of the ghoul are goofy and not sharp they don't hurt. The ghoul seems benign or silly and not something to be afraid of its eyes are loving. I also bought a white wooden model grand piano, a life-like penguin, a bleak mock Tudor house, a toy photocopier, two 500-piece jigsaws for my daughter and some realistic rigid animals to crap punctuation about the apartment. The toys I like best are the bits of toy that are the most prosaic or the most like human ruins. I turn them over in my hand as a giant alien emissary might. I got a plastic red brick wall with a grey plastic mantel, a very simple and beautiful thing a gem of a find. I also got a taller and thinner plastic red brick wall that when you press down on the top bit bursts into three big jagged pieces of wall as if a car had ploughed into it or someone got busted out of a jail. Then you can just click the bits of wall back together again and do it again. I think it's incredible engineering for children. We did drag the charred chassis of a motocross bike home from where it'd been dumped down Stocky Bottom and we set it in a contorted arc across the hearth. It was surrounded by other things: thick springs and discs; sheeps' skulls and jawbones greening on the mantel; dangling xylophones of smoothed driftwood fingers; dark petioles fanned suspended on invisible threads pinned into the Artex ceiling; framed skeleton leaves when I was a child. This instilled a sense of beauty to me in me. Insistently gorgeous kinds of death bounded homeyness. Nowadays I like arranging bits of crap stuck to the walls at home. I staple-gunned the made-up cardboard box for a Japanese mechanical money box to the wall of the living room quite high up. There is a used negative lateral flow test Blu-Tacked to the lintel as you come in like a mezuzah or garlic. I like putting up postcards and photocopies and rubbish. I elevate things just myself. There's: a red and white plastic analogue clock for dementia patients that tells you the day of the week you're in; a Valerie Solanas' SCUM postcard next to a glossy still from Pippi Langstrømpe; a postcard of a painting of a white cat bathed in sunlight by Géricault; one of Dad's geometric mountboard wall relief things coloured with blue and green oil pastel; a card bookmark with an old drawing of a funny orgy on it from the Sade show at the Musée d'Orsay; a painting of a grinning black cat I did for a version of pin-the-tail-on-the-donkey once; a sheet of A3 copy paper that sags with the weight of: a knackered pale pink fabric flower on it and a box unfolded to its pattern glue-gunned on it by my daughter; and a postcard of Tim Hunkin's papier-mâché automaton doctor all on the wall in the dining room above her iridescent roller boots and a fibreboard doll's house we found in the street now filled with wrinkled conkers and there's the interminably uninstalled set of smoke detectors in their boxes. I'd like to get my hands on a jeweller's loop; I'd scrutinize plastic toys' surfaces through it less and less. I prefer postcards of paintings because I am very possessive and the way I appreciate a painting is as an image for me, an inspiration never on its own merit. I don't go in for postcards of sculptures at all. My right hand convulses when it has to hold something carefully without support. I'm right-handed. The convulsing will start gently but can quite quickly build to either a wide horizontal swing or a tight elderly glitch. It's unstoppable actually unless someone else acts quickly to remove the thing from my right hand. Then I can drop it to my side to reset it then, my right hand I'm haywire. I can't carry a full glass in my right hand because that hand will convulse and fling the contents of the glass everywhere but I can draw very detailedly as long as I can rest my hand and my wrist on the surface of the drawing while I do it. The convulsing is actually from forever tightly gripping pens and pencils when I draw. It could be alcoholism or a brand of arthritis or related to the buckets of nicotine but I think it's the gripping-pens-and-pencils-all-life-long cause. I remember sitting with Andrew at a bar celebrating something and we'd just been poured two brimming coupes of champagne but when we raised them for a toast my right

hand threw mine all over us both, all over the bar.
I remember carrying a mug of hot lemon drink down the
corridor and halfway through my right hand chucked hot
lemon all over my hand, the walls, my legs and bare feet.
I feel the convulsion coming but there's nothing I can do
to stop it. I most often just stand there and take it. I say, Oh
no. Photos of my children are too much for me. I teeter
above a hole looking down at a photo of my children on
the phone. They're dead. I don't know what to do my children are dead. Photographic representation hauls a
semi-transparent plastic thing like the hard oblong in a
squid from me, a canal. Photographic representation renders corpses and my feelings so tweaked slip to hysterical
quickly because photos of my children that I see are a his-
trionic parody of my beautiful real children and my
feelings mirror that parodic shrill for what may as well be
real. I meet realistic representation on those terms without wanting to, particularly when I'm a long way away
from getting corroboration, proof of life. Images and I
shadow one another and the dance is quite complicated
and smeary. Being realistic enough to the world and to
myself is as close as it currently feels I can get to an exter-
nally relatable reality as a condition of truth so it is that
blasphemously modelled grief is similarly basically real
and the scandalization subs for very real grief in my feelings sometimes. Feelings can do that, can't they, they can
sub for one another. Depending on the current vivacity of
belief stock, writing this feels vile. My children were not
dead the last time I saw them mere minutes ago but every
time a photo of my children is taken corpse editions of my
children do slip heavy from a vent to the floor in: the
corpse sector. I can't get to the corpse sector but it is
optionally infinitely real. I can think about the corpse sector and focus on it and attain an incredible level of fidelity,

can't I. I can zoom in to see even the weave of a sleeve or the maggots' faces. I can imagine anything but I mainly imagine this kind of thing. My parents were made safe by my picturing the neverending procession of their every awful death but my powers have now mellowed to ineffectual vestige, sadly freed but I nevertheless picture it all, the multiversal tragedies unbidden self-mortification. There are regions of my brain. Tears come for artificial things. I weep for music and for movies and strangers. I am always aware that with weeping there's always an observational dispassion that is further in or out than the thing that does it, me. When I'm set in crying mode my directive is crying. It becomes hermetic and sadly it won't remember why it is. Crying that's lost like this can turn into a frightened spaceship with a solar sail that's golden. After dinner I used to convincingly mime chainsawing into the limbs of or slitting the throats of my terrific family who'd obligingly jerk in agony and gurgle to death it was a wild glut of love after eating beef stew! I liked to say chickenwithgravyandpeasandjacketpotato as fast as possible, my favourite. I do a convincing chainsaw with my mouth that can benignly double as a motorbike for my children. The chainsaw is for something else. The motorbike can go from dawdling putter to obnoxious rev. I am a Super Recognizer. I a hundred percent know who it is from just a peep in reverse three-quarter profile even, say, and at a big distance a person I have seen just once before but I would flatly refuse to work for the police if they asked me to. The more precious the thing I'm carrying in my right hand the more likely I'll shake it to pieces when the convulsion comes. The convulsing is not only muscular but quite psychological and supernatural. It's a staged intervention by an inner me differently evil than the top one that writes the more or less sensible prose or that cries out. This inner me is a slick right arm and a crude hand and that's it. It can slip into my upper right hand like a vet into a cow in a stop-frame from inside and then write with my top hand language in the air in red wine or hot drink. I can't risk pouring anyone anything with my right hand. I confess it did get to me. People politely watched me shake their drink about the place. They, the people, looked concerned. They thought I was nervous or I am an alcoholic. I don't want to have to explain anything at all to anyone ever. I want it easy with my friends unless I can control their responses and control my reception of their responses. I realized that I could pour and carry liquids and do other necessary mechanical accuracies with my left hand instead and no one need ever know about my right possessed one. I draw incredibly detailed things with my right hand sometimes, incredibly detailed skin. When I sense the convulsion coming I have the presence of mind to turn away from the laptop. I'd rather soak or scald myself than anything or anyone else. There's no trust inside. I heave sighs like Dad did not of relief but submission. I could be Salieri from Mozart. I don't finish spoken sentences much they taper off most often in optimistic and necessary anticipation of someone else taking over, so writing to people is sometimes just a way of having access to statements' end, saying no. In speech my sentences will taper to wordless implore that has to be met compassionately to be anything. I get flustered if mutely rebuffed and will compensate by agreeing to whatever. I contort all up and thumb myself into the wild appeasement slot. Stoppering the wild appeasement slot with myself is a different way to stopper a feeling. I am adrift if someone's a discrete wall and they don't want to join in with finishing my thoughts with me. I most often can't make statements through my mouth. A museum director ridiculed me and my hilarious charismatic unintelligibility on a stage in Düsseldorf once. I was answering his questions sincerely and heartfeltly and enjoying myself. I was improvising and exploring new ideas live but this left me open and so after a while he smiled at me and raised his palm and interrupted me to say sorry but that he hadn't understood a single thing I'd said. He had no idea what I was talking about at all and I fled. I'm anxious about being baffling to others especially at a point when I'm trying to give an account of myself or my work and especially, worse, if I'm enjoying myself doing it. I need bafflement shared and put in the same place by everyone present's hands and be a pleasure stealthy. I don't like it when my pleasure is converted to shame by others forcibly. I do want to be inexplicable but my language locks me out of others' affections, sadly. I have just ordered a gin and tonic but they have no tonic, sorry, so I plumped for a cup of orange juice with ice and a gin miniature and I have just now poured all the gin in we'll see how that goes. I try to have a gin and tonic on flights. On flights I cry tears for me not visibly and turned away to look out of the splintery window listening to my music. Oh, I'm folding inwards again. Pretence and truth of me are indiscernible to me and I fret over this. Whether what I am saying is true and where. When I start speaking I am astonished by what I say sometimes but it could be the astonishment of revelation or appal I have no clear way of knowing and no one else could settle this for me ever. A ventriloquist was diddling with me on his lap. I got ventriloquized by a dirty ventriloquist. I try to get the window seat on a flight because I don't want to be disturbed and I have an incredible bladder. I want to wallow instead. I want to be straight-jacketed for it and silver padlocks and buckles tinkling up there.

Brown leather creaks when it is tightened. I'm trapped in my body and the captivity of flight models that in a way that makes it easier to be very upset about. No-one knows about the pilots. I can be outside of myself enough to be compassionate to myself on a flight. Like everyone I like thinking about how people will react to my death. I think a few people will be caught off guard. People don't think of me as someone who is dead, people think of me as someone who is alive. People don't assume I'm especially alive but they can't know I'm as contiguous with death as I surely am. People think I'm a person unremarkably alive like others. I like to think about afterwards without me. Sally keeps a list of the music I want played at my funeral on her phone. Music's sentimental license or enquiry-exemption makes it best for getting in big transferable sadnesses. Just before everyone rose to process from the church at the close of the funeral the appositely serene dawn opening of Rossini's William Tell overture began only it wasn't, it was Spike Jones' version that segues quickly from harp and violin to cowbell, bulb horn and gargling and the extended family looked scandalized a bit. I ask Sally to add music to her list when I hear music I think should be played at my funeral or at the wake. My power comes from being born evil, a lifetime of projected consolation. I can withstand and do anything. I was designed specifically for pains some pains. If a piece of music captivates me I listen to it repeatedly and the music and I bundle till unremarkable, even detestable to one another. One curse of passive vampirism or not passive but irresistible is like all vampirism just vampirism not mirrored, rent open. I realize the feeling a piece of music teases by listening to it over and over. I get closer with each listen to a point of mistaken identity. This is different than thinking music is about me this is mutual. Music wants its heart found and mine too, in turn, for it. I weep with music because I am the same as it, and where it goes I mourn and envy as if I could, too. The extra trill just once in the second movement of Beethoven's first piano sonata pitters up and the small skull of my heart stirs on the pillow in the cot in my chest it jiggles on. My loving is also insatiable supping till all you're doing is you're cradling a husk. I'm dependent on having my feelings pressed into service. I wrote a very short will when I was nine: I leave my telescope to Rupert. I thought about Rupert looking at stars their light refracted by tears. I do now, him then, at least, love. I like thinking about how other people will react to my death. All the precarious things will topple I have nothing prepared. There are pubs and bars I have been to a lot about which I have no idea what the inside of the toilets looks like whatsoever. I'm aware of whomever I'm with's toilet-going frequency because I just don't really ever need to go it's pretty much always optional. They leave and come back and I just sit there. Sometimes someone reports the remarkable decor of a toilet in a bar to me and encourages a forced visit. It's not conscious anymore I trained my bladder when I was eleven. I wet myself on a school trip when I was eleven and for a while afterwards I needed to be close to a toilet at all times just in case. I stayed home from school for a week practising resisting the urge to go for ever-longer durations near enough to the downstairs toilet in case, sometimes just hovering outside the front door in my pyjamas in the cold, not going, receding into myself again and looking at the snake's head fritillary and the empty milk bottles awaiting collection. The dull pain ebbed so. I busted something in me then and my body stopped trying to tell me it needed to go. It just found more room for piss by getting rid of other stuff. It told me about the transposition of some pain. There was an astronomer whose bladder blew up and he died of it while listening to a king give a very long speech, which connects the telescope to my deadening. When I did go back to school I was extremely powerful I still have it. I'm a charged steel box. I'm open. I can mill hurt. Of course I do still need to go sometimes but it's more or less a formality. I'd like to send a drone or a probe into my childhood. I drink as much as most. I have noticed that a person's need to go to the bathroom often seldom correlates with the quantity of liquid they're drinking. I just looked up 'what muscle it allow you hold it in' and it offered the detrusor muscle which is under autonomic control. I looked up 'train detrusor muscle' which took me to a pdf titled 'retraining your bladder'. One of the tips was to sit on something hard when you need to go. It's what I do when I need to send a shit back up into me. My body's a farming machine you sit in. One of the secret ways I'm special is that I can will my body to do anything but I have no willpower. I have total control of my body but no way of choosing committedly what to do with it, at least unbidden. It must be bidden. I don't have control over my choices which are unrecognizable from one moment to the next. When I need a shit I can keep it in me indefinitely but it is worrying imagining the shit changing into something worse, poisoning me or fusing to the inside of me. When I choose to go to the toilet there's less shit than there should be because some of it is now stuck fused in me because of how long it sat there. It's the opposite of petrified by days. I caught myself at the fridge with a mouthful of bright yellow leftover curry, fake beer and vape at 11 AM I'm a maniac. I laughed at it at all of this this dazzling schmaltz I think I'm so happy and replete I could cry. When I'm sick people pay me compliments about how good I look.

Some sicknesses are beautifying. I'm exhausted. I have two small children and they're so special to me. I circle: a drain. I like very close-cropped bits of my face in the mirror well enough once I'm shaved but reports of what I look like given to me by others however I find extremely difficult to recover from an encounter with. It is clear that what I see when I see a photo of me isn't the same as what other people see when they see me but what do other people see where I see a criminal piteousness? Video of me's less awful than photos because each frame passes too quickly to entirely corroborate my ugliness even if another instance of my ugliness inevitably replaces the previous one and so on, the constancy of difference between each frame deflects the concentrated scrutiny that convicts me and prevents the infinite ugly amassing loop. In videos of me a part of the looking is given over to time's mutability just being expressed which in itself isn't ugly or beautiful but in its indifference lifts things free of final condemnation. In stillness I'm monstrous but I make a pretty sort of sense in faint motion. The motion of a sleeper or a note decaying. Otherwise it's celestial motion so to us an unaccountable stir and not perceptible per se, the scale evades. People sense me in their periphery like a non-biting insect. There aren't videos of me running as an adult or anything like that but there are lots of videos of me talking and listening believably in a seat. Video confounds memory and I'm grateful for this. What I think is: what's remembered from a video is a compound buffed to shiny flux by memory's sentimental temporality. Memory makes visuals lenticular if it makes any visuals at all I don't think it does. When I remember something an image might come but if I keep thinking of it and zoom in on that image inside my brain it's not an image at all it's atomic essence. I like how my energy in videos of me talking is. I'm charismatic and ex-cute. People who have told me I'm charismatic have something I can't guess to gain by telling me I am but they are also actually uselessly right. One article about me said I have 'an almost hilarious charisma'. I have worried about what that means ever since. I have maybe a sense of what it means: I am laughable in my live entreating to join me in my devotions. I don't think deemed hilarious charisma alludes to something uniquely compelling about me but if it does it retractably singles out my emotional sycophancy as hilarious, sardonic, and that the invisible grovelling I'll do is repellently captivating. I am irrecuperably pushing commiserative and I make noises when I'm listening to someone whine because I want it in kind which is a normal contract. I like manipulating people to make them trust me. I never betray this nicked trust but it is founded on an erection. I have the sort of charisma sure that's really confusing its forcefully equivocal and billows messily into space. It's sick it's very unappealing unless you're into the like or are like that. You have to be saintly to accept me or be a real brick generally or a kind of Jain, or gemlike or soft as thistledown. Some people have reported to me that I am intimidating. This book is a cast of my back or a dead man. It's got pink petals bruised plum by the grab of a toddler, incessant love. Fake sentimental construction is safe for tears where real death is not safe it's francium. Real death pares lustre back to the mince or blows up everything. I like getting in my mech when it's in the hangar when everyone else is in the mess. Being alone with my feelings in the dark cockpit of the mech when it's off is an important time for me and when it's turned on the body of the mech amplifies me, my gestures and feelings, it even has an electrosensitive dermis that can feed erotic sensation back at a scale I can cope with

36

and protects me from sensations I don't want like the dang of trees against my mech's shins or the ping of a bullet off my mech's pauldron. I can be concealed and protected but really exposed at the same time in my mech. There's no actual cameras in the cockpit to see me but my every move is captured using nanobots and perfectly recreated by the mech massive. The lag is fractions of a millisecond so really good. I can butt a building down in my mech or wade across a sea with ease. I can feel the tickle of fish shoals recreated teasingly on my own calves but not the crack of masonry. The face of my mech is my own blown up a hundred-odd times in angled golden alloys that can deform with variable current passed through it and when I tear up spent fuel-dumps track amber smears down my mech's golden cheek corbels; when I put my head in my hands the mech's huge head clongs bell-like into its golden gauntlets with me in it and when I vocally berate myself in the cockpit the mech warbles and coos melodically but there's no equivalent for its shoulder-mounted plasma cannon on me – for that I can press a button to ace another, tankier mech. The weight of the world should be felt, I feel. Mine is a light-type mech with weak armour, golden and frivolous. All my credits were blown on cosmetics. Oftentimes my body's carefully captured by lots of sensors velcroed into elastic pouches at the joints in an Xsens Link lycra onesie and a pair of puffy Metagloves by Manus. An iPhone is clamped to the end of a crooked metal arm strapped to a rig round my head with the screenside facing my face at all times to use the built-in depth camera instead of previous methods where they'd put black freckles on the places of my face that corresponded to blendshapes in the rig. There's lots of normal witness cams about the studio space around me but just for cleanup and animation reference;

there's no visual remainder in the rendering itself which is important for allaying dysmorphia a shame. The computer-generated model of my body is as accurate a recreation as was currently possible with MetaHuman. My head and hands have been scanned meticulously by lots of cameras racked on a column surrounding me and then hi-res skins made from those photos mean the model of me's face is forensically accurate but my body had to be approximated by crumpling up a generic male model and sanding its buff off. The final rendering's very like me but unlike with a photo I don't find it paralyzingly repulsive I find it fascinatingly so and the difference between kinds of repulsion is very important to me it describes me. The double's an effigy I want to make suffer in my stead. I find it liberating to be able to do something about the repulsiveness rather than be stalled by my being inside of myself and incapable of apprehending myself. I like swapping that swollen term out for a pristine word somehow new to my personal vernacular but not necessarily actually new to me, if I can remember this is possible. I can't shake 'fat', though, and I say it about myself with such appalling plosive emphasis I can make myself upset enough to cry. Newly re-gifted words to use to describe myself change my life for the better if they're nice or benign. I have recently been re-gifted the word 'calm' after a long time of not having access to it for whatever reason. 'Calm' occurs to me easily now, anew and effectively for now. I know what it means and when I say I am calm it makes me calm. I can change my life like this, one word at a time. I can say that I'm calm sometimes now. The word 'family' was donated to me anew two years ago. Ian said that my videos were dead men. This is the number one personal catechresis ever I have ever been given. One of the greatest gifts of my life. Catechreses are my all-time favourite things, even if I didn't have a word for them until a couple of years ago. It's true, my videos are dead men. It is an ongoing tragedy that Ian died when he did. Like a lot of people I think about him all the time. I have barely known anyone who's now dead. I didn't really know Ian but I loved him. I can cry for myself but not for others, as the first is something I can make happen and observe, and the latter is something I wait and wait to have happen to me to no avail. I wept when Leo Bersani died I'm not totally sure why but it's to do with ambivalent self-knowledge and the desire to be an artwork, looking at myself weeping over Leo Bersani's dying. I like men born dead. You don't have to kill living men to make them dead; you can just use a recent computer to circumvent murder if you're fantastically me and birth death in moving imagery. In this bit men are born dead, as I have said. They're videos. I insist that some of my videos are dead men because it transforms the presumed things about video that someone might ignore into the unignorable astonishments of a corpse. And not the vagaries of the nominalized corpse, which does not account for incommensurable experience; my dead men are enchanted artificial corpses with a felt lack where a life might have been —my dead men are bogus, though, made dead to order and in order, in part, to model feelings otherwise unavailable outside of losing someone close to you for real. I like the profanity of making dead men. It's quite safe to feel things near my dead men; they're decommissioned and aren't real at all. The event of dying does not happen. This is all a boon of the excessive, disgusting realism in my videos and the fact that they're made of: data, then light. Tears are made crocodile by the doomed life aspirations of technologies of slavish representation. This is evident to those of us who are still alive I mean, your tears can be sincere if you like, and founded in your own truth if you have some, because accountability for the sham lies with the video who is the dead man I made. I am certainly a masochist, and maybe the most. I asked Martin if the word 'sadism' was from de Sade. The horror of death is massively tempered but still somewhere close by my dead men. Maybe neutered is what I mean; slowed to a tasteless syrup you can uselessly eat or touch because it's inert, which is a significant thing for art to do. Actual dead men's bodies were the first crash test dummies sent flying through windscreens I think and this is what I'm also using them for, my made dead men, for testing more or less tragic things out on. The men who are dead who are my videos are dead individuals named things like Even Pricks rather than Philip. My videos are also rubies turning slowly on velvety turntables but them being dead men is the best one. I have ruby bearings in me as a part of my clockwork but not that many, and I can whistle my ruby whistle sometimes as good as Dad did, with the vibrato and accuracy of no-one around any more. I can do a very loud whistle to get their attention from across a busy street or across the fields by using my fore- and index fingers on both hands, extended and pressed together, each pair of fingers touching the other pair of fingers at the tip of the index fingers in a V then pushed against the veiny side of my curled back tongue. It has to be those fingers and like that; I have tried other ways. Other people can pinch their fore- and index fingers together on one hand only and use that against their fold-ed tongue to whistle loud. I can sing difficult intervals a capella. Not much of the red colour inside me is from rubies; most of it is because: blood's everywhere, even about the rubies. Some people surely despise me they think I'm pretending, they don't buy it. I'm not sure about this perhaps I'm completely pretending all of the time but another person's disdain very wrongly assumes the pretence is a feint to cover a truth I have even remote access to regardless. I do not and I have tried very hard. I want an enema right now I want to be hollow. While the babysitter dozed in front of the TV downstairs I sat cross-legged on the landing picturing all the ways my parents die that night. If I imagined my parents' deaths in sufficient detail it couldn't also actually happen like that. The two reports of their deaths – one conjured by me in advance of the other, the real one, out there in the dark – could not both exist. My imagination would supersede reality and stop them dying. I'd perform this ritual until I heard the front door go, when I'd slink back to bed unseen. I was convinced of my apophatic powers, even though I felt certain I would fail. My parents just die in a manner I had neglected to imagine. The idea of failing to apply my divine powers properly is incipient. I'm a bad god. It had to do with a seeming adult overhaul of my imagination. Drilling what I thought was reality's truth while clinging to my specialness. Specialness tempered by experience didn't banish it it just became occult and destined to fail. I had understood that reality was awful. However pleasant or benign one's life, sooner or later something appalling would happen. Reality's revealed and my parents are killed. I thought the longer I was happy and feckless the more terribly reality eventually asserts itself and calls in the debt. Only my laborious magical processes stand a chance of holding it at bay. I still believe this, it's the source of my power, my depression. I dreaded accidents. Dawning preteen consciousness wrought a shame that whittled to prick childish conceits in a way that made terrible sense of death's inevitability. Destined for death and suddenly somehow culpable for my thoughts and actions, deadly accidents promised to teach a lesson that would finally banish innocence and usher in adulthood proper. When Dad did die years after it was protracted agony and of cancer and I had failed to imagine that. I am all the time desperately searching inside. I want to see the bright lights tonight. I like getting the most I can from a piece of music. My powers include close to death. My forthcoming death isn't a situation whose inevitable arrival will be the sole garnered circumstance for the final confession of rare and powerful feelings to others and to myself I can get there today, which is unlike Dad even if his terminal realizations were the truest. Melancholy is attendant, actually soldered on, but it protrudes backwards into me where there aren't nerve ends anyway, there's only the fantasy of the unverifiable that's mine alone not to be able to verify. There is my inability to discern the truth of what comes out, or specifically understand myself from the outside, the things about myself that are meant to be seen or heard or read by others or by me after the fact. This afterwards might be tiny fractions of seconds during speech while my mouth's still a bit open. When I have a cough it's dramatic. I push hard at a cough to make a big noise. I strain at my throat muscles. I shove at the silence door there until the constrained muscular thing's so taut that the sound I finally make when I open the door in me is very loud and resonant, wild. I like people to say, Are you okay? Yes. I'm okay. 'I have a beautiful singing voice and my mother can be destroyed by a glimpse in the mirror.' I have had the exact same cough since childhood. I have worked on it over time, actually. I have made my cough sound worse over time. I like to worsen things that can clearly and I hope safely take being worsened, I hope trivial things. I hope I look unwell and sound unwell but am not unwell. I don't care about muscliness I only wish I were thin. I mean I would want to be able to pick things up, pick children up and carry them or a box of books and walk a long way carrying, but I mean I don't care about the look of muscliness. When my cough gets going in winter it sounds amazing. I don't ever worry about it it lasts for ages, far longer than unsolicited advice recommends a visit to a doctor, yes. I reassure people. I tell them the truth. I don't suffer I reassure people. 'I'm fine.' I put a brave face on it it can seem but it's fine I'm brave in reckless ways rarely. I am comforted by my secret robotic godliness. I am thinking about an iron moon right now. I am in control of myself and subject to that control's externality, too. I feel sovereign and subjugated back and forth. I feel like a semi-autonomous thing lifting and dropping a big weight in a lab or like an iron moon. The atmosphere's sodium-streetlight-orange and people breathe out only they mustn't breathe in. With me it's a matter of turning something happening to me into something I am choosing to have happen to me. I can retroactively author my cough by italicizing it when it happens. I make bad things worse to pretend I wanted them to happen bad in the first place. I take a lack of control and draw attention to it and make it seem like I'm in control. My attention does it. I take control by transforming external causes into choices that I make. It's when bad things happen and when I'm trying to make artworks. It isn't about changing something from bad to good but about saying that I make bad things happen deliberately. It's likely I make art like this somewhere in there. If something good happens to me I don't claim it as my doing. That's not one of my powers. Nothing about any of this can change: what I am. As an awry god I make it all happen unconsciously as a mere consequence of being divine rather than as a scheme to improve my circumstances. Improving my circumstances is not allowed. I'm not in control of my hellishness it's not something I ever chose, negative omnipotence. I can see stuff seeping out from the soles of my feet. It gets everywhere; it gets on me too. I can't consciously apply my powers and I wonder if other gods go about unable to apply their powers. Powers escape involuntarily like untrapped wind. Interestingly, the way I perceive my mind is bodily. Specifically, fixity of purpose is physical force, it really is energy in my muscles. My bladder and bowels are shit-caked plastic tubs or plastic tubs caked with a Weetabix cement and with sweet room-temp milk puddling on the bottom of my bowels in browny-marbled puddles. I don't need to know an author's desires I just need their deliberateness to aerosolize pink around me. I don't know what makes it pink. I often say, 'I like obscure choice', or 'I like obscure, confident choice', or something like that. What I mean is that I like it when in a film or another thing something structural or very formal happens that's unmistakably deliberate but also inexplicable and unrelated to the assumed consistency of the rest of it. And then that inexplicable thing doesn't happen again and if it did it would worriedly ensure you understood the deliberateness and assuage rather than risk the thought of accident. Somehow or baseless. The risk of being mistook as inadvertent or ill-made is important to me for art to take. There's a scene in *Bringing Out the Dead* when they're eating pizza in the hospital and the camera's doing a normal looking at the two of them in turn then abruptly does a strange stepped orbit around the woman, dissolving between static angles on her, looking at each side of her as she pauses in speech doing nothing, naturally. The camera goes back to normal immediately after these few beats and it never does anything even remotely like it again. I like freak inscrutable authorial choices that explode procedural consonances like that. They point to an available infinity of creative possibility, even if a term like 'creative' is awful, and a type of immanent meaning that's lavish inasmuch as it is demonstrative of art-making. Also, marking choice opens a door to: great arbitrariness and grace too, a profane grace. I often consider a parabolic image of this grace shorn of religion: there's a beautiful person offering themselves to all. They gape, facing away from the direction in which they would receive an answer and they're singing, an absolute adonis, a shining sub, a successive meek doubled over and open to pain or love or, and so patient and seductive or repulsive. Some of my art is I hope like this. I receive nuzzles and little licks or terrible fucked-up-ness but it's not up to me to choose which one I will receive. This doesn't change my hope that I get licked nicely. *Bringing Out the Dead* is a criminally underrated movie. It suffered from being sandwiched between more noteworthy movies of Scorsese and came out in a year with stiff competition. It really captures the era and stress and characters in a very surreal way. I am now entertaining the idea that the most wonderful things spin fast in the air, catching the sun and flinging sunlight about and never landing. I like the idea of showing art in size order. I think that's a terrific impulse. All museums should arrange their collections in reverse size order. I think about it and things like that and I mourn the pre-emptive veto in the curator's brain a little bit. A specious, meritorious fear in others often fantastically confiscates how I like to experience art somehow. Legibility's very worried over. I don't mind not understanding something, really. Understanding is most often comprehension and not sympathetic awareness. It feels moot to my thing. It's just that unequivocal meaning's

monolith does pound innumerable small soft grey limbs'
faint digressive reach easily, they think, to mush. Some
people try to solve art's ambiguity with imported significance or with candid aboutness where the thing it's about
gives allaying eminence? Deference to worthier worlds
brings a backwash of instrumentalization, at least to me.
I don't like most everything to do with contemporary art.
Most everything that supports contemporary art is sick
even often the artists, too, and the art itself is often nothing unless trussed up to recognizability or purpose i.e.
interpretability for the sorts trying to swaddle it in their
sick. When I'm at a contemporary art thing I will look
about and I'll think I see a whole fucking edifice a whole
crowd of people who are bonded over a hatred arising
from a fear of art but they're all professing to love it, art.
I am an apostle of art. Honestly, and as ridiculous as that
sounds and for real, but it is quite something that a lot of
the people closest to art are often those most terrified of it
they tremble with the effort of restraining themselves
from kicking its head in. I like a specific and contingent
sort of irony that can't compromise sincerity but can loose
moorings, however strong the moorings seem. My desires
for art aren't possible and almost they're disgusting. I like
simple organizing principles to disarm more complex but
also way more actually violent ones. Like everyone I like
lists 'of things', 'top tens' of things. I like long numbers
that refer to unimaginable amounts or dates. I like that I
can type 'six million dicks' and they boing into existence
elsewhere and donk against one another like the magnified silicon bristles of a new kind of pastry brush. I have
always liked measuring things with end-to-end football
fields, stacked Statues of Liberty, Eiffel towers, elephants,
etc. I like line-ups of silhouetted monsters in ascending
ginormousness with a little obliviously doomed human

in silhouette at the end for scale. I'm shown lots of adverts on Instagram for mobile games where you play a tiny monster or minnow that you make eat smaller ones and every ten or so that you eat you transform into a bigger and uglier version of yourself, eating bigger and bigger fish and getting more and more big and ugly until the player's eaten everything in the sea or in the world. I like to measure the circumference of the earth in intestines and I like the stars I see to be long dead the best. I commiserate with excessive unimaginability, 'phew'. I can count very high but I get impatient so I skip big amounts of numbers in between the start and the end. I feel emotional certitude about everything but I mustn't speak of it. The ambivalence I like is performative like love needs sometime be. I do equivocation socially but in my heart I am certain. Art's ambivalence is a bluff to protect its unpronounceable certitude, where unavailability's coaxed into synonymity with ambivalence. It is about really adoring not knowing forever and ever. Aspects of me confuse other aspects of me and I'm at a lovely loss or just gone. This is another sign of my secret inadmissible divinity. I wish I were the single trill. I wish I were the pristine guitar drifting in at the end of 'Wuthering Heights'. I wish I were the saxophone solo in 'Zen Archer' or 'Love Weapon' but I am the wall of brass in 'Horkstow Grange'. I loathe being from somewhere. I do not wish to know who I am but I do wish to discover every detail only momentarily insignificant. Momentary insignificance should be poised to squeal out and clamber over machine-chamfered significance. I like the hi-hat closing every few bars in 'Dancing Queen' it's like a spangled toy steam engine slipping into the past a beat at a time. I am the first Caprice. *High-precision ghosts.* 'Someone died in the night. Lost my fountain pen.' 'My pain in my spine is bad!' I didn't used to do hot drinks save for hot squash. I did hot Ribena and cold Diet Coke for caffeination till I was in my mid-twenties. A hot Ribena and an untoasted onion bagel with nothing in it for breakfast at college in the mornings. I liked how hot Ribena flushed stolid bagel clumps down into me. Blackcurrant is often the incredible flavour of thing I go for when something comes in multiple flavours. If there's no blackcurrant I'll get rhubarb second, and so on. Most people like chocolate best but I don't, I like fruity. I have three top memories of times with just Dad. Number one is getting vivid purple sorbets cassis in waffle cones at night from a waiter at the service entrance of a restaurant by the river somewhere in Paris and walking slowly back with Dad beside the river to where we were staying eating sorbets cassis not talking but in love, I hope. At number two is him taking me to London Zoo before Christmas and getting me a roast with all the trimmings for lunch in the warm zoo café and watching the flamingos through the big window, pale pink lines in the outside cold blue. At three is him burping the alphabet on a wet walk near Grasmere and teaching me how to burp the alphabet and by the end of the walk I could do it. You swallow little pockets of air between each letter. You have to get air into your oesophagus. I regret learning how to burp the alphabet. I swallow so much air now when I eat I often feel uncomfortable. He could tap out the 'William Tell Overture' on his teeth with his thumbnail and he could wring his hands in such a way as to make them shriek like piglet-like things and he knew about birds and trees. His elbows had circular dents at their tips from leaning on drawing boards but the heel of my right hand is burnished from mouse use. Dad had to die to be remembered like this: scarcely and shining. I liked to have a half-pint carton of semi-skimmed and a few Marlboro lights from a ten-pack sat in the street before the camera shop I worked at opened in the morning when I was a late teen in Oxford. I prevail between generations that drank no water ever and that drink so much water. When I remember to drink water I do a lot to make it up. I like pissing clean when I piss. My top favourite piss to do is after beer. It's so much piss, a comprehensible relation of in and out and giddy; the pleasure is easy and long and there's something or nothing left in beer that makes its piss version clear and it seems extra quick to come out. My sight seethes at the edges while I go as if piss were fast-boiling where my piss-iris meets the black volcanic stone pupil. I hear it as a loud silence in my head when I go. I like that kind of drunk. Piss steam rose in a cold bog. I smile when I think of my friends. I like to change up my order in a bar throughout an evening. A big pils then two double gin and tonics then a little pils with a Jameson's chaser on a Tuesday after the children's bedtime at the pub on the corner with Steve. I just went to the 7-Eleven after the children's bedtime and bought a Smirnoff Ice, a pre-mixed mojito in a fancy faceted bottle, and a can of sweet cider with a tree on the can just now. I lined them up on the wheelie coffee table and drank them in this order: pre-mixed mojito, Smirnoff Ice, sweet cider. I poured them out in the same glass in turn; a glass meant for water. I wouldn't order any of these drinks if I had a choice. I was bent over my laptop writing into a word processor designed for focus and sucking on my vape loads. I have two other vapes the same that are charged for when this one runs out so I don't have to wait for it to recharge and be without vape for a moment. The TV's got *Horowitz in Moscow* on it from my phone and I'm playing the turn-based deck-builder Hearthstone on my laptop in another window than the word processor. I have only one earphone in so I can hear if someone wakes up and needs me. Horowitz is too quiet for what it is but that's okay; I'm watching it for the audience's faces and the camerawork. 'It must be said,' I like writing more than reading. I have never been into reading all of a long thing and sticking with things. I have read a lot but I have not finished much. When I read I read selfishly and patchily. I look for bits in books to reassure or inspire or something – it's never for plot. I have always found a way through life but I will threaten suicide quickly. I don't like this because it marks me as a kind of generic awful man catastrophist and a coward or a novice. There doesn't seem to be anything so important that I can't say no to it or back out of it if it comes to it. I am grateful to be asked to join in but I am sceptical of conspicuous opportunity and participation. I might have made good cover art for Kanye West but I don't think so. I thought the softcore pixelart gifs he'd made himself that he shared with me that maybe he wanted to use for the cover were stranger and better than anything I could have come up with. They were surprising. Despite my encouragement he didn't use his pixelart gifs in the end for anything, I don't think. I am inexorably shunted forward by the motorized wall I'm braced against. I move toward the world subtractively. I do know what I don't want but not what I do and that is a powerful kind of wanting. I am blessed mush. My skin's got heat-sealed crimped seams like a thick plastic bag of milk. My arm and leg skin is covered in keratosis pilaris all over and that's been a massive factor in finding myself repulsive. I say awful things about myself to myself often. I call myself a fat fucking cunt a lot not in front of my children but certainly in front of Sally. It's shocking but I'm fantastically upset when I meet myself in that way. I say incredibly horrible things for shock but not deliberately and it is to shock myself, irruption. Who? I have no talent for health I think finally I am not interested in my health but I would like to be thin just once. I am beautiful beneath the neglect. No more than a few centimetres down but sadly it is all about: the top part and the really inner parts, it's really hard. I don't want to die but I won't do anything ordinary about slowing it. If I want to look okay I must remain very vigilant at the controls I make sure my tongue is flattened against the roof of my mouth so that the corresponding mass between my chin and neck doesn't belly horribly. I begged and then shouted and then whacked myself really hard about the head with a plastic recorder. Then I threw the recorder at the wall and marched to the kitchen. Then I leaned over the sink breathing, trying to breathe it all out down the sink. I like the kitchen sink, the kind moron. I like being at the sink. I feel calmer at the sink and the same is true of the toilet. The sink and the toilet are more subs agape but it's also the surrounding parts you can rest on that do it for me. I would love to have access to a deep ceramic sink with a curved mixer tap with brass turners but what we have is a quite shallow stainless steel one with a loose mixer tap whose sieved nose is clogged with limescale so the water spurts and dribbles this way and that when it comes out it's okay. When I shit I raise my right arm hauntedly and I point at something that's not there in front of me. My wrist arcs and my index finger rises and extends as the oracle's might've. I'm the oracle on the toilet, a bit possessed and pooing. I like that kind of shitting that's strikingly emptying feeling. Some shits, pisses and cums make me feel thinner and so better in that way as well as the action way. I had to sit in the side room during Christmas lunch weeping and tensing I couldn't make it work. I like eating other people's leftovers. It's consistent with me for me to do that but I also just like doing it without feeling any need for vindication. I'll go round after a meal when everyone's gone somewhere else and I'll eat everyone's leftovers. I do this with a performative naughtiness like I stole in from the dark to eat leftovers. I like to eat her leftover bowl of milk-swollen cereal from the morning in the mid-afternoon at the sink instead of doing myself some real lunch. I like eating his rubbery triangles of buttered toast from the morning and downing his backwashed orange juice dregs. I ate a whole party's leftover pizza crusts in a pizza place when I was twenty or so and I ate the contents of an ashtray in a pub when I was fifteen. I also ate the head of a red gerbera there and sipped at the smelly vase water delicately like a Count. I did these things in front of people but I like to nibble plants in the park alone. I'm writing this bit in the studio; I have just cut myself on something somehow. Coffee makes me sleepy and I like this very evident perversity. I think it's a quite typical ADHD thing so I did a free ADHD test online and I scored very highly, excitingly, I have an answer? It looks like I definitely have ADHD. I like my hair when I take my hat off; my head's a found object, then. It's disavowable or any style there isn't my doing after it's been under my hat getting pressed oddly. I like my head much more when something interesting's happened to it that I did not choose. When I find my hair sticking up in weird clumps the difference between discovering that, that the hat's done that, and doing that to my hair on purpose is big. Mannered vanity or freedom and beauty. I like wearing clothes that are in absolute tatters. My brown shoes are without laces and the soles loll at the front and the heel's rubber layer's popped off, the whole top's scuffed and cracked. I like my acrylic black and grey cable-knit jersey that was my father's because it is far beyond acceptably distressed, I have no memory of taking it. Its current preciousness is a symptom of persistence and the entropic winnowing it comes back around; trash gets precious. This is one way you can get trash precious. I like wearing this fucked jersey with a white shirt underneath. One can see the white shirt through big frayed holes that look like woolly bullet holes. I'll wear this top pair with a pair of green cords with gold zips at the cuffs, the shape's a little weird they're generous around the crotch and bum and taper to the zipped cinch at the ankles. They were special when I bought them because of how much they cost and the design but now the crotch is blown, the cord's balding in big patches on the arse and knees and the drawstring in the waist's just gone they're more special now. I feel exactly right in them; I didn't do anything to them consciously. I have to hoick them up all day long and an incautious lunge or a squat can extend a tear. I like looking ridiculous in some way or other and if it's not comic tramp I want it to be something. I like oversize clothes because they caricature and so render nonsense or at least petty what I hate about my body. I do intermittent fasting sometimes because it seems like a level of simplicity that might mean I'd forget about it and have the good aesthetic things happen to me without my doing anything but I don't really do it much. Get me thin and effete. I am effete already but the oddity of my unattended body makes for appreciable ambiguity, even if the habit of putting myself there in men's clothes is difficult to stomach. I go without food by not being near it it can feel terrific later. I don't wear my black maxi pleated Comme des Garçons skirt much because it means dealing with groups of men finding me and saying things to me about wearing my skirt. I am a coward enough dismayed by this kind of encounter to wad myself back into at least in some way conventional menswears. I keep my joys at home where I dance with my children unbridled. Onstage I recite Gilbert Sorrentino's 'The Morning Roundup' over and over in quite wildly different ways and I sing songs within a panicky mental reach, which are occasional reprieve, I meet the gazes of the audience and sing at them with the houselights halfway up. Songs like: Richard and Linda Thompson's 'Withered and Died'; 'Feed the Birds' from Mary Poppins; and 'Not While I'm Around' from Sweeney Todd. After forty minutes or whatever tolerable duration's for sustaining this kind of awkwardness and paltriness and schmultziness I start up singing Purcell's catch for sad drunks, 'Under this Stone', and a choir secreted among the audience joins me for the public expurgation. It's glorious to me. It's cheap glory. I used to wear my skirt for this performance but the friendly suspicion expressed by some at the conspicuousness of this costume as compared to my normal one was and is an unanswerable non-posture, so in Berlin I borrowed an aptly beautiful wool men's suit. I am straightforwardly repressed by pre-emptive fears how cowed by my sincere sense of picking joy's flimsy ambiguity to do what others needs must see as weightily political but which I wish were sleight just everywhere. It says something about the scantness of the incoherence I claim for myself as productive that I choose to convey, the relative safety of it. I wish I wore circle skirts and dark lipsticks specifically and moved through public days witnessed with love and joy with no further questions. Questions don't open but slam hatches on pretty faces shut often, it seems to me. 'The Morning Roundup' is a poem about the heretical triviality of the continuation of quotidian existence in the face of dead loved ones, certainly, but also the staggering beauty of the sun on Saturdays, which is an experience of a sort of reverse but more real bathos. The best and the worst do strike those of us dumb. I perform selfishly; it's something of a ruse to scaffold my sexless kinks in part that would be otherwise deemed cynical and non-biographical by others, I think. The performance is given a new title each time I do it. Synonyms; Epitaph!; A Catch Upon the Mirror; Epitaph without the exclamation mark; and Fangs for the Memories, which this last is what I might have wanted to have called the survey show at Tate. I went with Martin to install a video in an old abandoned wooden mansion on Büyükada filled with decades of busted furniture and shit, sodden mattresses and so many bulging carrier bags of fabric and newspaper just trash. When we walked through the front door we simultaneously decided to touch nothing more than we absolutely needed to: move nothing, position nothing, entirely resist the urge to turn a chair just so or set a door ajar or get rid of some incongruously pretty or inconsistent bit of decor. It was obvious that shifting anything, however innocuous seeming, would change everything; it would spoil the whole thing. Any touch would erase the history of the place – its actuality – and replace it with silly fiction, silly desires. I used to suck the bathwater from the flannel in the bath as a child and put the toy rubber shark's toothy mouth around my penis. I'd swill the dirty bathwater in my mouth for a bit, not swallow it then just let it trickle down my chin like a stone toad water feature would. I like pinching single beads of nectar from the white crepe trumpets of dead nettles by the roadside in the summer. Later in the summer I like plucking blackberries along the same route. It's a miracle to me to eat this sort of stuff, to remember to eat this sort of stuff or just encounter them and remember that you can eat them now. They're infused with exhaust and dusted with road and crop smut. There were yolk-coloured chanterelles crowding under the trees in the Engadin but it was a monochrome of inkcaps and puffballs on the lawn at home. I whisper to myself, 'What's it called?' with my fingers hovering over the keyboard or standing still somewhere, looking at nothing. My mind's not gone to a wrong thing but to nothing at all, just a nothing faintly charged with nominal query. I scrunch my face up and whisper, 'What's it called?' I say it aloud whispered a few times looking down at nothing at all. Sometimes I'll go too far into this asking and it seduces me away from the purpose of the question into repetitious void or I'll notice I'm there not remembering anything at all. It can come on suddenly, a nothing come surging up and getting a hold of me. It feels maybe like when you look in the mirror as a child and, making eye-contact with yourself at a distance to render a 1:1 scale, say quietly, 'I am me.' I can be in a flow of action too much succumbed to personal divinity and I'll stop dead and have lost the name of whatever thing and also have lost everything else about everything, too. Lots of things slip my mind and when they sometimes come back they often pretend they never left me but they seem happier actually. They seem happier and there's no down left on them, now, they have mauve grazes on their angles and they're lighter, sort of translucent, the nouns, when they come back, discovered anew, I needn't have worried about having lost them. Typing the wrong word into the search bar and then deleting it and then typing the same wrong word in again and deleting that again and so on, malfunctioning for ages until a spark fires deep in me in the dark and I turn over. I can be rebooted with an unk-inked paperclip inserted into this tiny hole at the nape of my neck you depress a dot. When I say a word wrong to Sally I'll say it wrong over and over like I meant to say it wrong and to funnily drive home the wrongness. I like the wrong to be engraved on the interior walls of my skull. I'm a potato fiend. 'It seems inevitable you'll become a Christian,' says Sally. My conviction, even masked, shocks me, even. Most of the time I hide how important the things I make are to me. I hit diffidence squarely and correctly smirk. I pull love back from the cave mouth. I like to put my cigarettes out in the food. Here's my cigarette, driven slowly into the icing on my cake with the cigarette going a loose z-shape and a tiny crazed crater opening up in the matt icing like a cartoon rocket's nosecone crumpling up when it bonks into an iron moon. Here's my cigarette being wrong again, dipped into the hummus and here it is dunked into my gravy on a round white plate. Here's my cigarette hissing out on meeting the water in the toilet bowl. I like tipping food I do not want any more down the toilet. I only tip foods down there that seem similar to what's meant to go down there. I try to be careful about fats going in the sewers and contributing to wet-wipe-feathered fatbergs clogging it up. Heinz Lentil Soup is the best soup. It comes out of the tin in one slow go, making slurping sounds as it goes out. The lentil soup smell fills the air instantly and is maybe the most tinned-food-smelling food smell of all time. The debossed ridges of the tin are visible on the sides of the loosed cylinder of soup that's doubled over in the pan. I heat it up without worrying the cylinder and the cylinder slowly resigns it collapses into just soup, a very thick liquid. I stir the soup with a short wooden spoon I particularly like and I stop thinking about the tube anymore – at least until later when I'm rinsing out the tin. That is when I think of the tube again. I have my small paring

knife I have held on to since I stole it from the cutlery
draw at home when I was a child. The handle's wood with
golden rivets riveting the tang to the wood handle. The
handle curves away from the palm aloof. The blade has a
slightly scooped bit on the upper edge near the tip I think
it's perfect, a perfect knife. Heinz Lentil soup is institu-
tional plus subtractive. It's just the result of ingredients
and processing and the economy of that. That's it. This is
what you get and that's it. I will say that it doesn't invite
love, but who wants toadying soups? Lentils can I suppose come off as lifestyled for health in the wrong hands
but Heinz are the right hands for me. I could eat so much
of this soup that I really like even if I lost all my teeth and
all my strength were sapped and my money spent and I
was propped up on pillows extremely ill. I'm very lucky
like that. I could eat it in a basement or in a field or anywhere, really: here comes a hot orb of Heinz Lentil Soup
in zero gravity. I like making out like cooking tinned
foods were high gastronomy in my kitchen. I like to present my cookery show. I throw conspiratorial looks down
the lens that's not there. I quip with my non-existent
beleaguered producer. I'll describe how to make my lentil
soup I'm making in the manner of a TV chef. I fold hot
sloppy soup into itself in careful figure eights as if it were
a meringue. There's a big Robert Rauschenberg tray of
sparsely bubbling mud that I think about when I look at
the soup heating up now. It was made in collaboration
with Bell Labs and Rauschenberg got to work with leading scientists of his day and had great funding to make
this deep metal tray of bubbling mud. This is the kind of
collaboration between science and art I like to see. I don't
like collaborations between science and art though I have
benefited from the sham of it as I have benefitted from the
sham of other ways art is painfully afforded by more

apparently legit domains. I liked this concert where these six percussionists played up on these little rostra all kinds of percussive instruments to a click-track, I guess, in their earpieces that was inaudible to the audience in the centre of the space. It meant they could do these incredible waves of rolling snare, for example, that moved like waves about the space it sounded like these mechanical reverse war waters. The precision was astonishing, actually thrilling I love that sort of thing, precise and virtuosic lunacy. It was really something even though there was a fire alarm going off in a neighbouring building repeatedly sometimes but it was Venice, too, so. Afterwards someone breathlessly told me that the glitchy, loopy noise recording that played in the middle of the performance through a PA that the percussionists miraculously played in perfect sync with was the sound of pulsars and I intensely disliked the whole fucking thing then. It's disappointing. Here it is: lentil soup from a factory after all. It's lentil-coloured with orange bits in from the past. The appeal for me is it's sick. I would eat it 1000x times. When I'm walking about outside an image or a phrase often bloops about in my head like a bloop of blood but it's mostly the rhythms of walking and breathing that mostly fill me up when I'm walking. There's not much room for thinking when I'm walking I just lightly touch the controls of my body when I'm walking I barely graze the controls. Micro-rhythms make a tight culture in my veins, synapses and breath-musics bridge recognition and an auto-intercession it's subtle, quite something. I listen to my part-authored body orchestra when things feel possible, when I'm buzzing and with a hiss my pneumatics vent at zebra crossings. If I stumble even once it's all over. I prickle with sweat and panic and the mechanical consistency's gone and the perfected beautiful me scuppers to meat again I go gross. I like losing my body and finding myself – not contained but jubilant. Sometimes this can happen. I like hiking in the mountains. During days hiking in the mountains I do breathing and I shape silent rhythms all day every day. I'll pause and smile at Martin or make an awed noise looking at the breathtaking sights that is the Alps. I like being an artist because it's an understandable thing to do with my time for my daughter. I have been doing realistic self-portraits of myself in red crayon on sheets of A4 legal papers and that is something she can understand it makes sense to her. I can wipe stuff off my fingers inside my trouser pocket and make a grotty cave. I like picking something up in a supermarket and putting it back elsewhere I don't want it. I have put a little bit of effort into a performance for surveillers but sometimes I'll lift a pack of fish fingers from the freezer and march to the breads and put the fish-fingers with the breads. I like to steal something from the supermarket when I do the big shop and eat something small and sweet while wandering the aisles like I'm on holiday. You can use the self-checkouts to steal expensive wine for cheap if you know what you're doing and you're confident of the person whose job it is to come over and okay the machine's query's apathy. I don't squirt petrol into postboxes and set the contents on fire when I see a postbox with its mouth gormless but I always always wonder why that doesn't happen more. I'm really great at spotting places to survive the zombie apocalypse but no other apocalypse. Inconspicuous places with a little height and they should have chain-link hemmed fore-courts for my group's shit nascent agriculture and I'm great at eyeballing great sniper positions for picking off zombies from with headshots. I'm trying to keep a low profile from myself. There's a poison capsule in my molar that a secret dentist hid in it for me. The way I do it is I flick open the hinged top of my tooth with the tip of my tongue and work the poison capsule from the hollowed-out molar with my tongue then I bite down on it while a big goon pins me. The capsule splits and a poison powder inside froths out like sherbet and goes in me. I fit and bleat and die then, while the goon's fingers are in my mouth trying to wrest the capsule from my mouth but it's too late it's not a capsule any more it's turned into poison lather and isn't reconstitutable. My secrets die with me. There are no secrets there is only the puzzle of fictions inside me, a blue crate. At this moment my life's truths' and fictions' indivisibility in me and to me maybe effectively erases them for good and I'm left with only my impalpables. The need for coherency's bits to be at least notionally supportive of other bits in a system to cohere or be possibly definitionally coherent is just not happening in me at all. I don't at all feel supported by my impalpables pussyfooting. I don't know what they look like or what expression they wear. Masks of worry. Their committed support awaits a nice shape from me regarding who I am. This from me would, yes, support them, my impalpables, but ambivalence or commitment's permanent deferral being integral to what I am or who I want to be is unresolved and the whole pronominal thing and its infinitely tassled hem may just break up in acid that I am the gas coming off of, I think. Poor goon's slumped beside my body dejected with their fingers slimy and flecked with pulverised poison capsule. I killed myself with a poison capsule eked from my tooth before a goon could torture my pretend secrets from me. There are secrets, actually, but they do not deserve the mystery or importance conferred by torturous extraction. I have this hardback on my shelf with a loaded pistol set in a pistol-shaped cut-out in the glued-up pageblock. I assume I can use guns in this. I like working myself very hard I can't ask for help. If I find that there's a tea or a coffee or turmeric stain on the white Corian I like putting a gob of bleach on it then going away and coming back after about fifteen-twenty minutes and wiping the bleach away and the stain going with it. Just before I wipe you can clearly see the stain's been freed from the Corian by the bleach. It's been raised up in the bleach spittle by sheer chemical actions. Let's say that the stain's ghost is caught inside the bleach foam which ate it up in a way. I'm looking at past errors through a repealing chemical scope. The miracle of bleach is the kind of miracle I like. I like obviously scientifically explicable occurrences my personal perception of which as miraculous is a condition of my ignorance rather than a conventionally divine intervention because it makes ignorance a contingent for my own personal divinity. I witness miracles because I'm divine, but the miraculous aspect is my dumb. This says something about stupidity fuelling my hubris and skewed reasoning for my lack of self-perception. I will leave ignorances that describe my extraordinary self-invention in a roundabout way alone and not rid myself of them ever. I always disliked learning if in any way obligatory. If knowledge is stored elsewhere or had by others and has no direct relationship to my personal pleasure I can't get myself to get into it, to also learn it. Other people describe deeper, deferred pleasures attained through long-form learning or the incrementalism of ordered and measurable skill acquisition but if something doesn't appeal to my wants for beauty or perversity I can't really care enough. I can't really describe how dispiriting chlorophyll is to me as an explanation. For me it's all about dough proving a warm tummy, for instance. Yeast is alive I can prevail. It

62

doesn't help me to think about what yeast is and what it's doing there; bread happens and without my knowing about how. I must do less than nothing; I must abstain from knowing anything. The closer clothes, food and so on get to my body the more repulsive they get until at the very last they're irretrievably condemned, they go crumbly and grey. I like to bring food up to my mouth and feel it start to vibrate more and more and then suddenly turn to filth on the spoon just as it passes the event horizon of my mouth which is a place just past my lips. I sometimes use the word 'repulsion' to mean becoming repulsive as well as prompting a sense of disgust. I have bought second-hand shirts and reawakened ancient body odours buried in the pits with the warmth and mug of my own body. I think this is a sincerely liberating dissipation of my edges. I wrote the words 'necromantic pine' to mean something like a yearn to bring back dead love, I don't know. I drifted an inch above the streets of Rome at night. My legs pedalled warm air too slow for the speed I was moving. I was crudely puppeteered by: hands in the dark. I was a long Pinocchio rough-hewn in a cagoule dangled just above the surface of the streets of the old occult Rome at night. My gloss red shoe-feet pretended to touch the ground but trod warm nothing except they sometimes went clonk against an ancient stone protrusion. I worked nights processing tacit familial mass to a yellow talc with my wooden teeth. I'd try to let the talc sift down through my bole and out my trouser leg onto the streets shiftily but my bole and everywhere was caked in bright yellow; a lot got stuck in me. On contact with the streets some of the powdered family mass turned into big ponderous black moths that went ahead to hug the streetlights ahead so I could stay in shadow and do my work disavowable. When we had to stay in Rome for longer than we'd planned because of complications I'd head out after bedtime and pound or just walk the streets and talk on the phone to Ben about picturing myself as a crude Pinocchio Machine made for processing unacknowledged or intractable upsets and about other things too and, so as not to censure a public with either my grotesque appearance or the work's ignobility or that glimpse of what actually needs to happen for a redemptive dawn, this had to happen at night. I was the patron saint of marionettes and threshers. Nighttime industrial urge. I like how it feels in Rome the most out of anywhere I have ever been. I don't feel relevant I feel wonderfully ransomed, pretty and trivial as pure pleasureman rubbed up and down against the stone, buffing butter furrows in the sunk floor of the Pantheon; mine own at the arrowhead of 2000 years. I like Rome in the revelatory cross-section, like a big cake again. I don't know what sweet crude's at the bottom but you can pan the camera all the way up to my red wooden feet clattering against one another above the surface. Fossils and stone buckle iron plate below, and the plies of glittering emerald hermeticism seep divinity into the groundwater and up to me. I think the occult courses upwards, attracted to my corresponding divinity. Just before dawn I pirouetted on the tip of one of the city's obelisks with my head thrown back ecstatically or otherwise drooped slack, let go by the big puppeteer, and the black cloth moths swirl about and obscure my face like my face is alight. I was often in the Pantheon with rain coming in the oculus seldom. I remember the countless gone performers' dormant stinks clotted the pits and gussets of the thousands of opera costumes I borrowed to thicket my installation of animations in Berlin. I remember a thing in a film where the villain had got his heart hidden in an egg in a nest on top of a mountain; that way he could not be

killed nor ever love so he's merciless. I always think of it
as Cope and Hagen, with Hagen being a mysterious thing
I can ignorantly survive. My boxers end their tenure
unaccountably shredded as if my crotch was brambly. I'm
not very active and I don't wash myself much or that thor-
oughly when I do unless I'm staying in a hotel room. I like
to take a scolding bath in an okay hotel when I can. I hav-
en't figured out how to ask for a bath. Some people don't
like taking baths because they think of having a bath as
just lying in a pool of lukewarming water dirtied with the
stuff one is trying to clean off of oneself. Those people
like showers because the water coming out of the shower-
head and cascading over one's body is always new and
whatever is dirty on you comes off and goes down the
drain away. I do sympathize but showers and baths are
false equivalents. A shower is an efficient way of cleaning
oneself especially if one is in a bit of a rush but a bath is a
relaxing way to really be if you have nothing really coming up and cleaning is more the bonus it depends who you
are. I like soaking, sweating in the tub. In the tub I like
how bathwater floods neglected crevices and frees caked
body sediment like a tide gently sucks sediment of shell
and crab limbs from rock pools back out to sea the bath.
One thing is that even though I lie with dirt and sweat in
the water I don't think the dirt can reattach itself to me. In
the bath I archipelago my body: my knees and toes and
penis and though I can't see it without a mirror my own
head as the principal island, the only inhabited island in
the archipelago. You can think of your eyes and mouth as
'inhabitants' for this. Pubes thatch a mangrove forest or a
reed bed, lapped by water turned brackish by sweat and
piss etc. When all the Radox and bubbles have wasted it's
a greenish Bonnard lens distending my body silly. Rising
from the bath one can feel anew. You have sloughed off: a

great burden of a day. In Germany there is a prohibition on public warmth. I like quite straightforwardly beautiful landscapes and architectures to conspicusouly falter in. If I can see something without the use of a mirror I can love it. Back in Germany now and the ads on TV in the breakfast room are for men's incontinence pouches and Meta VR, brown and purple right next to each other and the toilets with what we called inspection shelves in, a plate to catch your shit? Everything can seem bad in Germany but despite the resemblance I do not feel at home in Germany; it is my role to be awful so that other things don't have to be awful. I rely on my discrete masochism at least as it appears to me in me, propped up staring openly at a kingfisher, say, inside. My specialness is scuttled in Germany and in England; there are no kingfishers to look at nearby, I don't think. I'm too much a match for it in places like this. I would like to be the terrible detail in the splendid Poussin. It is a way to distinguish myself to myself that really doesn't work if my surroundings and I seem too alike even if we are not but seeming. I don't like where I'm from for this reason; it's key to my divinity to not be from anywhere at all. Distinction, even and especially dismal distinction, is important for me and everyone else. I have never been legitimated or otherwise by external diagnosis once and this has its upsides and also its downsides, too. I can cook up explanations to psychological problems or feel like I am or have something diagnosable that exists somewhat corroboratively and feel sated by the internal papering-over, risking neither the relative unquestionability of clinical recognition nor the more probable arraignment of what I thought was the problem. I fear discovering there's nothing wrong with me as much as I fear discovering there is. That's not true. I do not have an eating disorder until an authority affirms that I do but to me I do and it's mine to overcome or worry over as I see fit. I like all aspects illegitimate. What kind of eating disorder is this? and an answer is always an inherited determination and so an erosion of detail so why give it even if detail means ultimate indeterminacy? I don't really like any kind of thematic group exhibition unless the theme is acute and also oblique and the works have been cast against type somehow or their inclusion is novelly insightful or plain sleight. I was in a group show titled *Teen Paranormal Romance* once and I liked that. I can only function like a hermetic thing if I feel sure everyone else does too. If it were provably untrue I would submit to the lathing in a heartbeat but it's impossible to find out. I want to adverbalize words that don't usually get to be. I want a long line of people gesturing to the next saying something lovely about them. Not directly to them but to be coyly overheard by them. Lovely enough to make them blush and smile a bit. Then that one would gesture to the next one in turn and they'd say something lovely about the next and so on I wouldn't want it to ever stop. There's no one exists outside of the line everyone's there and the only audience to observe the lovely said is the recipient's internalized fantasy of a public clocking news of unsolicited declarations of their inimitable loveliness. This must not be instrumentalized or bidden. I like giving compliments freely hopefully without even secret grounds. If you can sincerely think of everything as a machine good for you. I have not mistaken luck for deserving ever, even though as a god neither applies above love's existence. How could deserving exist outside pat justification for privilege or a lacquered privilege bestowing meagre recompense? I add blue or black food colouring then to most foods so I can thrust food into a gutted future and gobble it sacramentally. I have changed. I know who is going to die in television. I like compelling games to play on my phone like *Vampire Survivors*. You only have to move the character around with your thumb the game fires your weapon for you at regular intervals that you can make shorter by levelling up passive multipliers. My favourite character to play as is a silly caterpillar called Sammy who starts off already with the evolved form of the cat weapon. The unevolved version is cats appearing and disappearing and roaming about you killing enemies but it evolves into giant smoking eyeballs that sail slowly about the screen through crowds of enemies killing a lot of them as they go. It's impossible to tell how they're killing things with what. It can be buffed to make the smoking eyeballs massive, numerous and faster. The caterpillar starts OP like this and its unique characteristic is that rather than gaining experience points for levelling via the usual blue, green or red gems that drop when enemies die, the caterpillar gains experience by picking up coins and the giant smoking eyeballs actually generate coins when they kill enemies, too. Plus, unlike with the gems or the other pick-ups, you don't need to be near the coins, the eyes make to pick them up and they get automatically sucked towards you from anywhere on the screen that they appear. I like to play as the caterpillar because you can get it so you're levelling up very fast the more enemies are onscreen being ploughed through by the giant smoking eyeballs. Plus, if you pick up a coin-spree special or something you get so many coins with every enemy death you can level up faster than the blink of an eye. Every game of *Vampire Survivors* is thirty minutes and by around the fifteen-minute mark with the caterpillar character you can already be at such a high level and levelling up so fast that the giant smoking eyeballs and also any other weapons you have picked up are so big and devastating and fast that they fill the screen, the smoke billowing out the back of the giant eyeballs obscures a lot of everything. One can just set one's phone down on one's lap and watch the caterpillar idle there in the centre of the screen surrounded by devastation done. Tons of enemies are killed every second and they can't even get anywhere near you while you just continue to get more and more powerful without doing anything because, again, you don't have to get near coins to pick them up as the caterpillar character and coins are what level you up as the caterpillar. It gets exponential super fast. At the thirty-minute mark every enemy spontaneously dies they don't respawn and a grim reaper comes so fast at you from nowhere and kills you and ends the game. With a good freeze build one can actually kill a grim reaper but even if you do so eventually an ultra grim reaper comes in. It enters from the left of the screen and moves very slowly across the screen towards your caterpillar character while the camera zooms slowly in on you and when the ultra reaper touches you you die no matter how levelled-up you are unless you're running the game in endless mode in which case it never comes and you can grind endlessly, I think, but curiously I have never turned on endless mode. You can also revive and get extra points or money for each revive. There is a cake passive that will increase the number of times you can revive. But this final ultra grim reaper will always kill you immediately after you revive if you're not in endless mode, I think. The things you actively do other than just move your character around in *Vampire Survivors* is choose weapons when you level up to a maximum of seven weapons and seven passive effects. The whole game's very passive, really. Each weapon can be evolved in its own right by collecting the right passive. There's a lot to choose from at this point after there have been a couple of okay DLCs released. It's a couple of years since the game first came out on many platforms. Some weapons are normal like throwing knives, whips and an aura of garlic, and others are stranger, like bouquets of flowers that you fart out behind you as you go around the map. The best way to play is to select weapons that sync with each other. There are other coin-generating weapons than the cat weapon/giant smoking eyeballs that can even make the levelling up speed of the caterpillar character even quicker. If you're playing with most characters using the freezing build you can get the giant icicle weapon which freezes and does good damage and which, when evolved, has a special where a magic ice symbol slots together in the centre of the screen and does a devastating screen-wide AOE attack. Also the legendary clock lancet (!) that fires freezing lines outwards rotationally clockwise second by second. This can be evolved into a powerful ice ring by getting a silver ring and a gold ring that are at the northern- and southern-most ends of the map so quite time-consuming to go and get. The silver one buffs you and the gold one buffs the enemies, interestingly, and picking up each ring spawns a very powerful enemy who follows you around and can very quickly kill you if it touches you. You have to not touch enemies if you can. Each map has these rings and also two red arrows facing left and right at the most easterly and westerly points of the map that are similar to the rings and also spawn powerful enemies when you get it. The red directional arrows are the evolutionary passive condition of a sprig of healing herbs that evolves into a little red cloak that saps the lifeblood from surrounding enemies at intervals. Not really a weapon, though it is a choice to make on pick-up to go for it. The caterpillar doesn't change its look with additional things.

Importantly you can move through frozen enemies without taking damage so when the screen's choked with enemies with the clock lancet there's always a way to keep moving so it's often good to try to get it unless even a minor freeze build doesn't interest you. When enemies are frozen the damage done by other weapons increases which can hold back the hordes that come until half an hour's up when a grim reaper comes and kills you with a kiss. Steam says I have put 952.7 hours into *Slay The Spire*. These are the ways I like to be touched and to touch: I like kissing so much. I like to be held tight then loose then tight again; I can choose to feel it as the start of a rhythm and constriction feels great in a way it's like being breathed for you, not even having to breathe for yourself. I like to be constricted in lust her teeth clenched, I feel the brink of loving violence every tautening. Run me over make me flat so all the loam exudes piles slowly silent out the end of my penis like a granular brown toothpaste inattentive passers-by skid in. 'Turn me into a street.' I like to be held and to be unsure it will ever end and if so in what way. I could suddenly be let go of off a building and drop like a coin into a wet slit. I could get squeezed to fossilization, couldn't I. It can feel when I'm held like it may never end. I like time to clench around me for millions of years in serenity. I like to be caressed to soothe rather than excite so that excitement is emergent it's an unconscious bodily usurp. I like her kisses the most. I like her tentative touch forever. I don't like being massaged. A category of touch that functionalizes care or for money but has no love in it even though it feels as if it does is: not what I want. Its proximity to grace is of course a burlesque of grace. I want the circumstance to happen collaterally and not be made to happen to the masseuse and me, to give and receive pleasure not because that's equitable but that it could do away with exchange altogether. To be able to reiterate simultaneously so that it can be the private condition for brazen self-abuse of another as if they're me. I mean that the doubling means touching another as touching oneself. Nothing should stray even a little bit towards debt and perhaps the best massages are like this. It is probably also a matter of the performance of sufficiently modulated gratitude expressed to a masseuse while being massaged, the right noises drifting up from the underside of the face cradle. The same thing is true with doctors and nurses. Reporting the effect of their professional touch regardless of its inspection is a complex thing as it presumes translatability, especially if the reporting is not explicitly asked for but given to vainly dissimulate. I really do like being touched but entirely practicable touch makes me feel stupid for wanting the doctor to be a lover. I have never had a massage. The personal lexicon of pleasure's expression can be colloquially infinite why not. I want to celebrate the doctor in their professional successes but also steer their touch to its limit. I want to let them know they're going in the right direction with their exploratory attention, that it's really great what they're doing but also allow myself to succumb to their authority and their confidence that doesn't need my assurances. My affirmative noises are gross and hilarious and mechanics roll their greased eyes, but I'd have to go in the first place to find out. My eyesight's astonishingly good I must be immune to deterioration and to death. Mutual masturbation where both parties stimulate the other and are stimulated by the other one or if not like that like a tool-assisted solo where one's a good tool for getting off. I could possess the frigidity to be a tool actually perhaps yes, I could be the good boy toy and the dildo's pleasure could have been mine if I'd not been fitted with inhibiting code. I am all for necro-robophilic futures or my dug-up fossil used as a dildo. My ancestors were all dildos. I want to be a butler and to remain a receding stranger to everyone, hollow and pretty as a foil-wrapped Easter egg. I'd like to have the white dress gloves on even when holding my penis. I'd like to sleep in a cell under the stairs liberated from personal attainment masturbating at night. I actually am not that stable or reliable outside the moment with a particular kind of other person who needs me. If my oligarch told me to plan their skiing trip I couldn't do it well it wouldn't be a good trip for them. I forget the very things I mustn't forget. The more consciously I instil the thing not to forget the more likely it is I'll forget it. I forget all names really but I can never forget a face. I don't answer the phone I just look down at the phone in my hand and watch it ring sometimes for ages. There's definitely an answering service on the phone but I have never checked it. There are lots of once-urgent messages from friends on it desperate for help who are now dead because I didn't pick up the phone when they called. The phone also makes corpses. Lovely voices thrown down it feel as if repeat broadcasts from a car crash dash cam sound feed. If it's a stranger on the phone to me they're the killer. I have nothing to say to the dead but that I'm sorry for it and the silences on the phone then that I should fill with inquiry or account instead seethe with a distant grief noise. I'm often speechless while I listen for telltale off-mic horrors their end. Stifled acoustics mean buried in a wood coffin and big reverberant ought means rape in a nighttime forest. Sometimes I have visions of awful things but a lot of the time it's superimposition from the poor genre cinema I like to watch at night on lookmovie2.to which has everything: *Evil Dead Rise*; *The Pope's Exorcist*; *The Purge* films; *Arcadian*; *Malignant*;

the one with an eyeball freeing itself from its owner's socket while they sleep and flying around witnessing the world's atrocities and returning to its socket before dawn back under the lid, and the owner thinks its nightmares they remember throughout the day eventually they go crazy and after more they go on to invent the internet. The phone is considered a gadget for chit-chats and catchups but nowadays for many it's all about the apps. Smalltalk is beyond me unless it means shrill, baffling redundancy because I can really lean into that. The weight of most kinds of sociability sets me on my knees and pulls open my arse as I have said. People who know me know not to call me. If the call's from those people I'll answer because it could be life or death for them. If I needed help with something I wouldn't call anyone I'd send a text message. I can actually cope with scheduled calls but bumping into people on the street is worse than anything. My trembling right hand precludes the possibility of a lot of hospitality and service industry roles for me. I would pour the tea over my oligarch's big son's ripped lap for sure. I don't know what the fantasy is but it has persisted for a long while I still want to be a butler even only if or when everyone to whom I am really responsible is dead and responsibility can be converted to disaffected employment. When I imagine my family dead I think about going into butlering or becoming: a monk or killing myself with drinking. I am aggravated when someone brings a thing into my home with an expectation that I'll display it if the thing has display as its purpose save for flowers. It feels crazy to me to gift people things they have to look at all the time even if it's quite normal to do that. I got a black leather waistcoat and a cupboard from my parents when I turned thirteen. I like moving all the moveable bits of home around. I feel my life change completely by moving a thing an inch or even less than an inch. We were gifted a big spray of blue stocks when our daughter was born, which was very welcome. I don't like mixed bouquets I like: one good kind of flower over and over. I spent probably an hour arranging the blue stocks. I plumped for a long glass ex-passata jar as a vase on the floor and aligned it with the righthand edge of the living room window a metre or so into the room. I made the stocks keel a little to the left as you looked at it from the entrance to the room and didn't care about other angles or sightlines. Not much off at all just enough off and importantly imperceptible to anyone but me. I was after the discreetness of a spray of stocks that hadn't been made to do anything deliberately. The spray had the right separation and no real symmetry. 'Right' here means looking found as is. It's the symmetry of a good scribble for keeps, it said nothing about anything. I moved the inherited monstera a bit closer to the off radiator and rotated it too so that the largest leaf expectantly shaded nothing on the floor there and also gestured towards the end of the sofa nearest the doorway. I changed the postcard covering the hole in the wall to an unused *Las Meninas* one from the Prado. I liked how the petals came off over time. They haloed the foot of the jar and were on the brown floor in a blue. The petals got carried about the living room by eddies of air from our bodies moving quietly and realistically just a little around our newborn. When arranging things I want it to look like nobody arranged it. Rather, aleatory. It takes time to achieve this especially if you're the one deliberately doing things to the thing and also the one who wants to not feel the deliberateness. I can't not fiddle with most aesthetic things to try to undo the choices lacquering them. On receipt of anything everything one gets has accrued all kinds of manner and I need to touch it for ages to pare it back to the central accident inside. My touch can be daintily acidic. I like to lick the brush that has residual Quink in the bristles. It tastes like ink which to me tastes like the paper wrappers from Chewits. When I get in a hotel in my room I take the art off the walls and tuck it all behind places and I strip the bed of all the fucking cushions and blankets. Jim told me he likes to put the do-not-disturb sign on the door for the whole time he's staying and makes a nest on the bed but I like to come back and find the bed remade in the way I do not like so I get to strip it all over again. I like yanking the blankets out from where they are tucked under the mattress and hurling them and all the excess shit into a corner. I like one or no pillow plus duvet. The people who remake the bed during the day don't put the art back up. Steve and I came up with a play called *Two people attempting to place a penknife on a bed so that it appears as if no one put it there.* My daughter and I like playing The Fossilization Game. She's a customer arriving at the fossilization centre I run in California in the living room. I greet her obsequiously and tell her about what we offer we can fossilize to all tastes. We can go from a 60- to a 400 million-year fossilization and anywhere in between. She chooses the longest option which costs fifty kroner. She gets in my fossilization machine the low armchair. I go over safety protocols and make her sign a waiver and hand over a deposit. There are some conductive gels I have to apply then I carefully dot her body with electrodes. Rapid burial is crucial for fossilization so I pile up all the cuddly toys and blankets and more things on top of her which are the rocks and dirt with urgency then I slosh a drum of my proprietary chemicals over it all. I leave one of her hands poking out of the heap for monitoring and then with some ceremony I turn on the machine I say, 'See you in the Future, then.' which is our slogan. My machine applies an unimaginable pressure and heat with a loud whining noise from my mouth and then a long hiss and that's it: my daughter's fossilized. I admire: the fossil. Even after all these years running a fossilization centre I still find fossils very beautiful, I never get sick of them. I do a quick extra fossilization on the protruding hand once I have established it all went well and then I leave the room. Cut to 400 million years in the future and I walk back into the living room as a future human returning to earth from a colony near Mars, my dropship's in the kitchen. I'm wearing a spacesuit and radioing a commentary back to my people up in the orbiting cruiser. I move tentatively; even though I am a human and I know I'm on my home planet I am the first one to come back for hundreds of millions of years. There was a catastrophe. I pick up toys: corpses. We have a soft cuddly toy skull called Mikes. All skulls are called Mikes to my son. 'Hang on, what's this?' and I find Mikes and the fossilization centre's sign on the floor. I pick them up, gawp at Mikes then blow a film of dust off of the sign and read it aloud. I mispronounce it in a funny way because language is different now. Then I accidentally manage to turn the machinery back on but in defossilization mode by tripping over a lever or something and my daughter bursts out from under the great pile of toys and stuff and sometimes she's become a vampire and attacks! Another game we used to play is *How To Hide A Daddy*. Steve and I laughed a lot at what if the truth of teleportation was that rather than mysterious scientific dematerialization, instead when you go in the teleportation chamber a terrible threshing machine unfolds from the walls and frantically threshes you up into crimson slop and red mist and then some listless technician wanders on wearing a rubber butcher's apron and long rubber gloves and shovels and squeegees the slop-you into a white plastic bucket to be lugged to another location where you're reconstituted in something of a rush. You weigh less each time and your temperament will have definitely worsened. This is because they weren't able or couldn't be bothered to get all your blood off the walls and the floor and even the flecks of gore they missed contain essence of you. 'You've been teleported.' You must not remember the experience or you'll die of shock so they always deliberately leave that specific bit of viscera on the floor that would remember the secret agony of teleportation. It's all a massive secret that's kept by the teleportation companies. You can tell if someone's been teleported if you know what to look for: a crescent scar on the heel of the hand where the machine first snags the teleportee with the tip of one of its deployed scythes. In the industry it's called a TST: a Teleportee's Stigmatic Tell. It's a defensive wound but the interesting thing is that it heals normally rather than how the rest of the body does after the teleportation which is by using: nanobots. Nanobots are the only way to re-weld blood in the right way and make it look like you weren't shredded and splattered. All it is is ten cc of nanobot suspension gel squirted into the bucket of teleported you and you just warm it up a little to wake the nanobots up who get to work reconstituting you straightaway. Reconstitution takes max. ten mins and when they're done the nanobots suicide and compost in you, releasing vitamins and minerals and data you need to reconstitute you as who you were. The data they use is from a long form you have to fill out before you're allowed to teleport. For many years afterwards a teleportee's resting face is much more aghast than before and they scream or laugh in their sleep much much more than before it. Lovely men from my past. Lovely men from my past. Like lots of people, *Invaders from Mars* got to me as a child. All the things that purport to. Blood circulates. A medical situation could be a space of submission to erotic interaction but I think that's not what they're for. It's actually a different succumbing expected in situations like those. It's succumbing to authority and trust in them to cure you of it that's expected. Medical professionals essentially stop you dying they don't join in with a mutual yield to pleasure and confused sensation, the doctor's oath-bound not to go down that path. Maybe a physiotherapist isn't and can. I mean I can't be isolated in my intimate pleasure with another, I need them to also be enjoying themselves and lost in the same way I am, selfishly sufficient not to notice how grotesque I am so that I don't notice it. It has to be a game gone wrong where the wrongness is good and is a sudden eroticizing. Enough to overwhelm mine and really all grotesquenesses at least as pejorative. Sally pulled a shard of glass from my heel with a needle and some tweezers. A few minutes before I had resigned myself to life with glass in my foot, rewrapped in flesh and forgotten over time. The shard of glass outlasts the meat around it and even my coffin, then. It gets eked from the dirt somehow and tinkles tediously about the world for ages. Made legato by surf, poking into things, things like huge dogs, it becomes more and more opaque and tiny and indistinguishable from anything, mouse cataract, a nothing that was once embedded in my foot. Regrettable relief then when it came out just now that that can't now happen. At the end of the day it is good not to have glass in me forever but I have kept the shard of glass stuck on a square of masking tape and I hope that I find the right moment to drive it back into me. It was Pyrex from a smashed measuring jug. I demand to see the x-ray reveal accreted disregarded needs in the shape of an old key or the shape of my skull, a tiny replica of my skull in grey medical plastic embedded inside. One problem of touch is the shame I have about the consistency of my body, and how if someone touches me I will feel very sorry for them and their likely surprise at how disgusting I feel to them. Like with acquiring a taste for gelatinous foods in my mouth I have to acquire a like for my body's awful consistency or I should get on with changing it to one I do like like toned jacked. I have to not presume my repulsion at myself a fantasy of another's encounter with my skin and my fat actually being repulsed. Others love me. I often squander mornings because they're full of promise. Sitting in promise is a wonderful stilling and really it's not squandering anything to do that. I don't go to anything ever. I can't invent desire in myself but so much of what I think of as what I do is inventing desire in others, most often, I think, for themselves, which can't be true. This is one of my responsibilities. I feel no obligation to attend to things I'm not interested in but I do feel a need to insert myself into other people's lives, particularly when they are emotionally unreadable to me. It's not something I consciously want at all it's an involuntary emergency response the consequence of a lack of facility for disinterested engagement. Every encounter is a trial of pretty overwhelming ungovernability, pathetic. I can't control people or know what they want unless I offer everything and welcome them into a permanent and intimate obligatory relationship with me without their knowing, a bailiff's second family. Trying to guarantee love which is all I understand or debt. I want to be loved the most of all. Other people's children can be a nightmare they aren't yet reciprocally empathetic. Children's faces can often be voids my frantic appealing gets swallowed up by. Children's feelings aren't yet consciously driving countenance, of course; children can't give me what I need. They often don't look like they love me at all, and rather than being mindful of pre-social child inexpressiveness, or just that love isn't a facial expression, I run away like a child. I really can't cope with my children when they're sad but I have to. I like fake vomit and fake turds. I think I have a collection of great fake turds somewhere and I think I have the Bristol Stool Chart somewhere that I didn't in the end put up because the illustrations of the seven exemplary human stools from watery to separate hard lumps like nuts weren't good enough. I like shouting something silly repeatedly; I was just now shouting, 'Clog boggler!' repeatedly. I am moved by structure only. Before I watch a film I'll find the synopsis online and spoil the plot for myself so I can look at the film differently, but also just because I love reading synopses. The best writing is people writing a synopsis of a horror or sci-fi film online, and the best YouTube channel is the one where someone affectlessly reads out a synopsis of a ridiculous horror or sci-fi film over a super-cut of the film. I like the dead internet idea. I like the *Sesame Street* version of the Andrea Bocelli song 'Time to Say Goodbye' where Elmo's getting tucked into bed by Andrea Bocelli. I find the new lyrics astonishing and incredibly moving.

Time to say goodnight.
Lie down.
Here is your bear.

You've had such a wonderful day
Playing and counting to twenty.

Singing songs

And going to the park with your friends.

So now won't you give me a hug?

It's time to say goodnight.

It is one of the best artworks in the world. It reminds me of 'Where Corals Lie' and asleep as the end for children is a lot to take I suppose as a parent, but the teetering pile of joy and ache, parody and sincerity I feel is where I really can. My emotional responses skim choice to begin with. I brush my feelings with my sleeve as they roll on into unintentional commitment I urge them a little in one direction or the other and they wobble for a moment like an almost cut-through tree or something. I'm sensitive to the tiniest shifts of weight when it comes to feelings. I can hear the fibres splintering in a glissando: it's my son's lovely thumb running down the teeth of a plastic comb. There's when my centre of mass moves beyond my base of support. There's from composure to rampant unrelent. A commotion in the morning too near the front door where our neighbours might hear and be quite shocked. I am governed by principles of gravitational acceleration, torque and angular momentum, etc., but at the start of it I make a choice to go, it's true. Astonishing swears at an astonishing volume can be upsetting. I'm writing this bit in the very back seat of a minivan now and it's hard to tell that. I like eating walnuts and especially muhammara because it teases what I can only assume is my allergy to walnuts. My tongue goes prickly and numb a bit when it happens and alien. I get to touch the hem of anaphylaxis when I eat walnuts, I feel sure. I like licking cigarette papers, ice creams and sorbets, fingers, knives' flat planes. My tongue goes out and then comes back in with something on it sometimes just invisibles of flavour. My index finger goes into the tub of hummus and it hooks a blob out and then it sticks it in my mouth. I suck on my finger with the hummus on it and it tastes great. My finger reemerges almost completely clean, you don't need to wash it. I like sucking my fingers and other fingers. I sucked the fore- and index fingers on my right hand while I fiddled with my left ear with my left hand when I was a child watching TV for hours. I used to fold the main dish of my left ear in half and then thumb it inverted from the back so it went convex instead of concave and it would stay like that till I imperceptibly tautened my face up when it would pop back into its normal ear shape noiselessly. I could keep it inverted during *Quantum Leap*. I like suctioning onto the opening of the cardboard Calippo tube and making a vacuum to suck the slush up from down the sides of the main frozen column. The cardboard tube buckles with the immense pressure I can actually summon with my mouth. I like sucking on cigarettes the best, then vapes and then fingers. I wing songs for things, stupid songs for things and some stick. When there's porridge for breakfast I always sing

> Porridge! I like it in the morning
> Porridge! I throw it 'cross the window
> Porridge! I tell you where to stick it
> Porridge! I forage for borage in porridge

to the children. When there's overnight oats for breakfast I always sing

> Would you like a ride on my boat?
> (Yes)
> Have you ever seen this kind of goat?

(No)
I'll give you access to the moat
(Okay)
Just let me know if you like overnight oats!
(Yes, please)

to my children. The songs have easy melodies that are quite jolly, too, cadged improvised and riffed on from whatever mush of nursery rhymes and they are to be sung in a broad Scottish accent. The responses to the questions posed in 'The Overnight Oats Song' are spoken quite flatly by my daughter. Another one is just

Flip the—
Flip the fridge-freezer on its back

over and over again with fridgefreezeronitsback run increasingly together each repeat in a clipped forties British army drill sergeant accent more and more exaggerated. I need something else going on. I record songs when I remember to, and I send them over to Rupert, who sends me the same kind of songs in kind that he comes up with too. Another one of mine is

Tupac Shakur
Tupac should concur

and another is

Anything involving mustard

which is like an ad jingle. Another thing that's different and not sung but a nascent catchphrase Steve and Chris and I came up with is you chirpily saying to someone,

'Here's a quill!' The seeming inevitability of my becoming Christian is what compels my resistance to it; predictability is repulsive to me so Sally's prophesy is perversely productive. Inevitabilities about me to others are especially repulsive. I use the word 'repulsive' a lot, as I have said. It does mean being pushed away by a physical force and also it means an involuntary response set inside one by God. It's the inseparability of literal and figurative with words the ligation and the word is God. I am a natural. I don't like when I get stuck referring to myself with a particular term that's gotten heavy with denigration by reflexive overuse, and the irritation I feel with its repetitiousness and predictability as some unquestioned self-perception has turned into self-hatred. I can comport myself even if I'm very frightened. I don't like interesting facts given stated as such. Now I'm not interested; I am instead very interested in uninteresting things that are over there. I'd rather punish myself than be attacked by God. I promised that one of my videos and the accompanying piece of writing would give you a tumour if you watched it or read it but I wouldn't pull that stunt now. I have never been under the knife but I want to be under it. When they cut me open they're going to find tumours and bones limp hollow tubes like cooked rigatoni in my sink and they're going to find gallons of creamy fat, too. I'm often a grave very full of wobbly fat with all the bits of my anatomy trapped in it plus midges suspended in it and wires baled and tangled up in it and fritzing. I like that I can delicately touch my hand to a lamppost as I walk past and it'll kink and droop like a flower because I'm super-humanly strong. I like flipping cars over like that too, making cars tumble like acrobats down the street. It's so easy for me to do it and people like it when I do it. I can't drive and likely never will be able to. The point of having a car for me is always to have a little turbo fiefdom where you can smoke and listen to music, even stay the night or live. You can go anywhere. Pick up your friends you can bomb down the road and go anywhere, maybe stop off at the service station for supplies you can park up and get out, stretch your legs and walk around a place you can't get to otherwise. You can hook anyone's phone up to the stereo these days. Cars are like headphones, I think, if I turn the fantasy around a bit. Machines of fantasy or for maintaining a space of fantasy the promise. A reason I haven't learnt to drive yet and might never do that I tell myself is that I worry I wouldn't be able to stop myself swerving suddenly into the walls of a tunnel or ploughing into the pedestrians and the shop windows. It's so much faith to put in yourself to get behind the wheel of a car that you'd be able to resist ecstatic deaths. And there won't only be a few moments where you'll have to resist the urge to destroy everything with your car over the course of your career as a driver; driving is entirely made up of making the choice not to destroy everything. You have to have an incredible mettle to get behind the wheel. Everyone says it's not like that when I ask them what it's like to get behind the wheel, and some people even say that they, too, were worried they'd not be able to resist killing people or themselves with their car. But they say in actual fact there is just something that happens and all that horrible stuff flies out the window when you get behind the wheel. You will just find yourself getting in the right frame of mind and you will just find yourself driving carefully, miraculously, not in a constant struggle with the other appalling decision to destroy everything as you go along incredibly fast. After you're over it you can relax and listen to music and hold a conversation with your passengers. I'm not convinced this would be the case for me. I am a nascent lunatic, I worry. I am always fingering the alternative, the worst. It's noteworthy to me that the roads are not covered in death and destruction they're not strewn with blackened wrecks and powdered glass crunch and bodies that the remaining drivers have to scootch past. After giving birth and for a long while afterwards Sally would look at all the people pootling about in their lives and remark, 'Every single person was given birth to.' If I did ever learn to I would do the automatics-only test. Like the men in my family I like being a passenger very much because as a passenger I can: listen to my music and read my book and doze off with my head juddering pleasantly against the bus window. I like to wake up a little on the bus and see stooped giants lumbering on the distant horizon, convincingly hazed by atmospheric perspective. Being a passenger is perhaps a significant bequest. I don't know what to pray for or how to pray. You are supposed not to pray for yourself or for something beneficial to you specifically or something that seems magical and far-fetched beyond the far-fetched magic of prayer itself. You're supposed to pray for others to pull through but I only ever remember that prayer exists as an option open to me when I feel myself in a state of emergency brought about by my not being in control at all of what awful thing might happen to me personally. It's always urgent when I remember prayer so that even as I shut my eyes to talk to Him as a last resort I stop short because asking for help with my personal emergency is not what prayer is for so whatever appeal I make would be ignored at best and at worst punished. Even if I tried to coat my selfish ask with a virtuous, generalist gloss, asking for something good for humanity, I know He'd know what I was up to and make sure the thing I wanted help with went wrong for me to teach me a lesson, punish me.

He'd probably make sure the platitudinous ask also went bad, too, just to make a point to me about my selfishness, and then the whole world would suffer as a direct consequence of my duplicitous, selfish prayer. This coil of thought gives a person insight into my battle with evil in my deified sense of self; God punishes other deities particularly lots. Consolations and. Better to be exiled from the garden of mercy than cower in the shadow of His displeasure. I'm texting this sentence to myself on the toilet. My phone buzzes and I already had forgot it was me that messaged myself, so I check the incoming message. I don't think it's forgetting I think it's a small haywire flit, a synaptic broop just for a moment and it's any excuse to look at the phone. I smile on the bog with my phone in my hand and then I perform. The text message thread from me to me is a sarky echo it's how I send myself ideas and also sweet nothings with inbuilt formal parody. You never know when good ideas will come to you. A similar problem as prayer is genies, how you have got to be very careful with how you phrase your wishes otherwise you'll become a cautionary allegory again and possibly destroy the world because I just wanted something good for myself. I want music! I try to encourage arrogance and pretension, relative to it all. All of this and more but it is undeniably hard to get God off your back if He suckered on uninvited years and years ago. I never talk to God I punish myself for my internal infractions and there is a little comfort in the will of that, how I get to hold the lash. I reach for prayer only in circumstances outside my capacity to affect them at all, so not being able to do prayers to God has never been a problem. I am often full of joy. I have been teleported before but the telltale scar is nearer the wrist than it should be and might actually be from when Mum plunged the garden fork into me when she

was turning the soil in the garden one summer's day and I
stuck my hand out under it for some reason. I don't
know. It was hard but I had an amazing time.

Illustration credit

'Untitled'
Ed Atkins (2024)
Red crayon on A4 yellow legal paper
Courtesy of the artist

Acknowledgements

Parts of this thing were published under different titles,
such as *Excerpt* or *Copenhagen*, to accompany exhibitions at
Dépendance in Brussels, Cabinet in London, and Gladstone
in New York. A section was performed for Courtplay at
Hartwig Foundation in Amsterdam, and early versions of
the opening were published in *Cura* and *Fieldnotes*.

Thank you to Steven, Martin, Chris, Andy, Simon, Ben,
Rupert, Henriette, Andy, Sally-Ginger, Hollis Pinky and
Gabriel Sophus.

The authorised representative in the EEA is eucomply OÜ,
Pärnu mnt 139b-14, 11317 Tallinn, Estonia.
hello@eucompliancepartner.com
+33757690241

This book is printed with plant-based inks on materials
certified by the Forest Stewardship Council®. The FSC®
promotes an ecologically, socially and economically
responsible management of the world's forests. This book
has been printed without the use of plastic-based coatings.

Fitzcarraldo Editions
133 Rye Lane
London, SE15 4ST
Great Britain

ISBN 978-1-80427-174-2

Design by Ray O'Meara
Typeset in Fitzcarraldo
Printed and bound by Pureprint

fitzcarraldoeditions.com

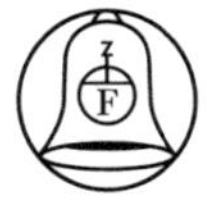

Fitzcarraldo Editions